Y FICTION DUR

Durst, Sarah Beth.

Out of the Wild

# Out of the Wild

# Out of the Wild

a novel by
## Sarah Beth Durst

razor
bill

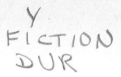

RAZORBILL

Published by the Penguin Group
Penguin Young Readers Group
345 Hudson Street, New York, New York 10014, U.S.A.
Penguin Group (USA) Inc., 375 Hudson Street, New York, New York 10014, U.S.A.
Penguin Group (Canada), 90 Eglinton Avenue East, Suite 700, Toronto, Ontario,
Canada M4P 2Y3 (a division of Pearson Penguin Canada Inc.)
Penguin Books Ltd, 80 Strand, London WC2R 0RL, England
Penguin Ireland, 25 St Stephen's Green, Dublin 2, Ireland (a division of Penguin Books Ltd)
Penguin Group (Australia), 250 Camberwell Road, Camberwell, Victoria 3124, Australia
(a division of Pearson Australia Group Pty Ltd)
Penguin Books India Pvt Ltd, 11 Community Centre, Panchsheel Park, New Delhi –
110 017, India
Penguin Group (NZ), 67 Apollo Drive, Rosedale, North Shore 0632, New Zealand
(a division of Pearson New Zealand Ltd.)
Penguin Books (South Africa) (Pty) Ltd, 24 Sturdee Avenue, Rosebank,
Johannesburg 2196, South Africa
Penguin Books Ltd, Registered Offices: 80 Strand, London WC2R 0RL, England

10 9 8 7 6 5 4 3 2 1

Library of Congress Cataloging-in-Publication Data is available

Printed in the United States of America

*For my father and my daughter*

Praise For

# *Into the Wild*

"*Into the Wild* is VERY cool, with a unique look at the great fairy-tale characters. I couldn't put it down until I knew how this brave, extraordinary girl could face such powerful magic!"

—**Tamora Pierce**, *New York Times* **best-selling author of** *Terrier (Beka Cooper)* **and** *The Will of the Empress*

"Sarah Beth Durst's *Into the Wild* is fabulous in the oldest, truest, and best sense of the word, harking back to fables, wonder, and magic unleashed. It's bold, sassy, and utterly engaging. I can't wait to see what she does next!"

—**Bruce Coville, author of** *The Unicorn Chronicles* **and** *Jeremy Thatcher, Dragon Hatcher*

"*Into the Wild*'s fairy-tale characters are fascinating, and Julie is everything one could want in a heroine—she's intelligent, practical, determined and brave; at once more ordinary and more extraordinary than she herself thinks she is. I'll be keeping an eye out for more work from Sarah Beth Durst."

—**Patricia C. Wrede, author of** *The Enchanted Forest Chronicles*

"*Into the Wild* is an entertaining, introspective, clever remixing of traditional fairy tales with a *Labyrinth* edge and a self-aware sensibility, and it signals a strong debut from Sarah Beth Durst."

—**Michael Jones,** *Realms of Fantasy* **magazine**

Thank you to all the fairy godmothers/godfathers who waved their magic wands over this book, including Andrea Somberg, Jessica Rothenberg, Ben Schrank, Tamora Pierce, Bruce Coville, Sara Crowe, Matthew Snyder, Jess Michaels, Pamela McElroy, Laura Schechter, and all the amazing people at Penguin Young Readers. Unending thanks to my family and friends, as well as my Book Ninjas Extraordinaire (you know who you are!). And a fairy-tale kiss to my husband, Adam, for sharing this dream with me. You are my hero and my happily-ever-after.

# *Prologue*

Warped through glass, she saw blue sky, a smear of leaves, and seven bearded faces pressed against the glass peering down at her. She tried to scream, and her lungs squeezed. Air! She needed air! She was enclosed: glass on all sides. She pounded on it. She kicked. "Let me out! Please, let me out!"

She heard a click, and the glass coffin opened.

"My Snow White," a boy's voice said.

The dwarves pulled her out of the coffin. "Run!" they shouted at her. "You can't let him kiss you! The kiss ends the story! Once he kisses you, you'll lose your memory! You'll be trapped!"

She couldn't move. She felt as if she were coated in concrete. Run, she told herself. Run! But the Wild had control of her.

Suddenly, the prince was there.

No! she tried to shout, but she couldn't make a sound. She couldn't even exhale. She fought against her own body.

Gently, he placed his lips on hers. She tried to pull back, to pull away, to stop, stop, stop! Inside, she was screaming and screaming, but her body didn't move. The prince released her.

"And they lived happily ever after," he said in an empty voice, a voice that Julie knew well—the voice of the Wild speaking through the boy's lips as if he were no more than a puppet.

Julie woke in a sweat. She tossed her blankets off and flicked on the light. She was home in her makeshift bed on the living room couch. She wasn't in the Wild. She was safe. It was over. Life was back to normal.

## Chapter One
# *The Third Blind Mouse*

Three blind and tail-less mice catapulted through the cat door, skidded over the linoleum kitchen floor, and collapsed in a furry heap at Julie's feet.

"Uh, hi," Julie said to the mice.

The cat door bashed open again as Julie's brother, Puss-in-Boots, launched himself inside. Close on his heels (or more accurately, hind paws), his girlfriend, Precious, entered the kitchen. Squealing, the mice scrambled over each other as the two cats beelined toward them.

"Whoa," Julie said. She jumped in front of the mice to block the cats. "No eating the Three Blind Mice!" The mice darted across the kitchen and into the living room.

Boots shot her a glare. "You'd make a lousy cat," he said. He and Precious ran through her legs after the mice. From the living room, Julie heard her best friend, Gillian, shriek over the beat of hip-hop music, *"Mice!"*

Oh, no, Julie thought. She sprinted toward the living room and saw

(1) three mice racing toward the TV,

(2) two cats bounding after them,

(3) one girl (Gillian, in a pink T-shirt that read, Northboro: Fairy-Tale Capital of the World) climbing onto the back of the couch, and

(4) a nine-foot grizzly bear executing a perfect pirouette in the middle of the living room rug.

Just your typical Saturday morning, Julie thought. And then she plunged into the fray. "Catch them!" Boots shouted as he bounded after one mouse. He pinned it against the ottoman. Precious darted after the second and third mice, who zigzagged underneath the coffee table. They spurted out the other side as Julie ran toward them. "Watch the bear!" she cried.

Jiggling one furry leg in the air, the bear lost his balance as the cat and two mice raced in a circle around his hind paw. Precious cornered one mouse against the radiator as the grizzly bear slowly toppled. "Julie!" Gillian cried.

Julie scooped up the third mouse and then sprang backward as the bear crashed down on top of the coffee table.

*Crack!*

The coffee table's legs snapped, and the table flattened beneath the bear. Magazines and remote controls scattered across the room.

Everyone froze, mice included. Julie felt the pat-a-pat-pat of the mouse's tiny heart beating fast against her fingers. The bass from the music continued to shake the room. The bear squatted on the carpet and danced just his paws up and down. Quiet movements.

Julie started to laugh. It's not funny, she told herself. Don't laugh. The coffee table was smashed. The mice were petrified. Mom would be furious. But she felt the giggle bubble up from the pit of her stomach. On the couch, Gillian began to laugh too.

She heard Mom's footsteps on the stairs. "Is everyone all right?" Mom came into the living room. Seeing the coffee table, she sighed.

"Sorry about the table, Mrs. Marchen," Gillian said. "He can't help it." She was right—the bear couldn't help dancing whenever he heard music. He was still under a spell cast on him while he (and everyone else in central Massachusetts) was trapped inside the Wild. Hopping off the couch, Gillian fitted headphones on the dancing bear and affixed an MP3 player to his fur before shutting off the stereo.

"Your mom was just on the phone. She wants you home for lunch, preferably without the bear," Mom said to Gillian. She paused, and Julie saw her read Gillian's T-shirt. Frowning, Mom said, "I'd rather you didn't wear that here."

Gillian gulped. "Sorry!"

Looking at Julie, Mom raised her eyebrows. "Julie, did you know that you're holding a mouse?"

"We rescued the Three Blind Mice!" Boots said.

"I see that," Mom said. As Boots filled her in on their heroic rescue (involving dumpsters, dogs, and a ride on a motorcycle), Julie helped guide the bear back to his "cave" in the basement and then walked Gillian to the kitchen door.

"Sorry about the T-shirt," Gillian whispered. "Do you think she's mad?"

Julie hesitated. Yes, she thought Mom was mad. The T-shirt reminded Mom that her worst nightmare had come true. Six weeks ago, someone had made a wish in Grandma's wishing well that had caused the Wild to escape. It had transformed most of Massachusetts into a fairy-tale kingdom, trapping everyone in its stories, before Julie was able to reach the magic wishing well and stop the Wild with her own wish. As the guardian of the Wild, Mom blamed herself for everything that had happened. She didn't need a T-shirt to remind her, especially when she was working so hard to encourage everyone to forget.

"It doesn't give away any secrets," Gillian said.

"Just please don't wear it again."

"I wish you'd trust me," Gillian complained.

I wish you'd understand, Julie thought. Something as awful as fairy tales didn't belong on a T-shirt. Why didn't

Gillian get that? Out loud, she said, "Did you bring the story?"

Sighing, Gillian pulled a folded wad of paper out of her pocket and handed it to Julie. It was a school assignment—they'd been instructed to write a story about what had happened when their town was transformed into a fairy-tale kingdom. (The school counselor thought it would help the students cope with their memories.) Julie and Gillian had planned to lie, of course, but Mom wanted to review both Julie and Gillian's stories before they handed them in. "Um, maybe you can wait until she's done being mad about the shirt and the coffee table before you show it to her?" Gillian asked.

Julie slid the story into her own back pocket to deal with later, when she wasn't holding a squirming blind mouse. "I will," she promised. Mom wanted to make sure there were no clues as to what really happened in their stories. She didn't want anyone to know about Julie's involvement or about the magic of the wishing well. And she certainly didn't want anyone to know that some of the Massachusetts residents who had been trapped in the Wild were actually *from* the Wild. Julie's family and their friends wanted everyone to believe they were ordinary people. Even without T-shirts or school assignments, it was, Julie thought, kind of an uphill battle.

Without warning, the mouse in her hands shouted, "Ring around the cities!"

From the living room, another mouse piped up, "Pock-eted by kitties!"

The last mouse cried, "Ashes! Ashes! We all fall down!" As if on cue, the mouse in Julie's hands tossed its head back and threw out its tiny paws like a fainting heroine in a melodrama.

Gillian grinned. "Call me later?"

"Sure," Julie said, and shut the door behind Gillian. Carrying the limp mouse back into the living room, she asked, "Um, what's wrong with them?"

"Aside from being blind, tail-less, and bad poets?" Boots said.

Mom frowned at him. "Poor things never recovered from their time in the Wild: chased and maimed over and over again." Julie shuddered and tried to shake the image from her head as Mom added, "The return of the Wild clearly didn't help their mental stability."

All three mice lifted their heads. "No, no, no Wild!"

Julie stroked the third mouse between the ears. "It's okay," she said. "You're safe now. The Wild's gone." Well, sort of. Okay, really, it was right upstairs, underneath Julie's bed, lurking like a leafy octopus.

And that, Julie thought grimly, is my fault. When she'd made her wish in the wishing well, she'd had the chance to destroy the Wild completely, but she had chosen to wish for her "heart's desire." Her heart's desire had been to have her normal life back. As she'd later discovered, for her, "normal life" meant: a father who was lost inside the Wild, a mother who was Rapunzel, a brother who was Puss-in-Boots, and the heart of fairy tales (reduced to a tangle of vines) under her bed. She, Mom, and Boots were back to being the guardians of the Wild, responsible for ensuring that it didn't grow large enough to trap people in its fairy tales ever again. And Julie was sleeping on the couch and having nightmares every night. Oh, and lying to poor, frightened mice.

"You're with friends," Mom told the mice. "It's me, Rapunzel."

"Rapunzel, Rapunzel, let down your hair!" the mice chorused.

Mom flinched as if she'd been struck. A second later, as quickly as if she had put on a mask, she was again the unflappable and serene Rapunzel. But Julie had seen the flash of pain on her face. Julie tried to think of something to say. Sorry I didn't save Dad. Sorry you had to relive your worst nightmare. Sorry our town is crawling with doctors and scientists and reporters and police who would love to discover that real fairy-tale characters exist . . .

"Rude mousies," Precious purred. "Can we eat them now?"

The mouse in Julie's hands trembled from the tips of his pink ears to the pale stump that should have been a tail.

One of the other mice sang, "Rock-a-bye, mousey, in the cat's paws . . ."

"No, you may not," Mom said to the cats. To the mice, she said, "We aren't going to eat you. We're going to take you home. Remember home? Your nice, safe cage in the library with that nice, sweet librarian Linda who feeds you—"

At the name Linda, all three mice squealed. The third mouse twisted violently in Julie's hands, and Julie felt a sharp pain in her index finger. "Ow!" She dropped him. "He bit me!"

Bouncing on the carpet, the mouse scurried across the room. Mom tried to grab him as he ricocheted off her foot and then doubled back toward Julie. "Catch him," Mom cried, "before he hurts himself!"

Hurts himself? What about her finger? Julie grabbed for him as he bounced pinball-like off her sneaker. She missed, and he veered toward the stairs. Yes! They had him! Mice couldn't climb stairs—

The mouse leapt. His front claws dug into the edge of the step, and his hind legs scrabbled behind him, propelling him up onto the first step. Okay, so maybe mice *could* climb stairs. As Julie started forward, Mom said, "Let him go. We're scaring him."

She's right, Julie thought. He was terrified. From the base of the stairs, Julie watched as the little rodent climbed:

leap and scrabble, leap and scrabble, leap and scrabble. He hoisted himself up onto the top step and then disappeared around the corner.

"He'll calm down on his own," Mom said. "He's safe enough in the hallway."

Right. He could bounce off the walls up there until he calmed . . . Oh, no. Julie froze. "I left my bedroom door open."

"Julie!"

She always locked it when they left the house! But on weekends . . . She'd been hoping that the Wild would decide to leave her bed voluntarily. Couldn't it live in a different room? Maybe a closet or the garage? Or even the dining room? So far, they hadn't been able to budge as much as a leaf, and she wanted her room back. "I'm sorry! But I'm sure he won't—"

"He can't see it." Mom ran past Julie up the stairs. "Don't move!" she called to the mouse. "Wherever you are, don't move! Just wait!"

Julie pounded up the stairs after Mom. "Mouse, stop! The Wild is up there!"

Mom halted in the doorway to Julie's bedroom, and Julie skidded to a stop behind her. "Everyone, stay calm," Mom said.

The mouse was less than a yard from Julie's bed. Underneath the bed, the green leaves of the Wild rustled as they shifted and writhed. One vine uncurled, reaching out past the dust ruffle toward the mouse.

"Don't be frightened," Mom said softly and evenly, "but the Wild is directly behind you." Piles of clothes, books, and papers created a canyon that led directly to the bed. If he ran . . . "Come toward my voice."

The mouse quivered. His fur shuddered in gray ripples. "No more knives. Please, please, please, no more knives." A leaf crept closer.

"No one here has knives," Mom said.

He inched backward. "Run, run, run, as fast as you can. You can't catch me!"

Another tendril of green snaked over the carpet.

"Stop that," Mom said sharply to the Wild.

At her tone, the Wild shrank back, and the mouse skittered closer to the green. "Not you!" Julie said to the mouse. "Do you want to go back to life in the Wild, back to being controlled like a puppet, back to living the same story over and over again, back to losing all your memories and everything that makes you who you are?" Julie had chosen to abandon her father, the father she had missed her whole life, rather than live trapped like that. "You have a life here outside the Wild, a home—"

"She knows!" the mouse cried. "She knows we know! She knows we know she knows! She knows we know she knows we know!"

Okay, he was totally insane. Who knew what? What was he talking about?

"You're agitating him," Mom said in a singsong voice. "Come toward my voice. You'll be safe if you come to me. I'll take you home to the nice, safe library—"

Squealing, the mouse tripped over his hind paws in his efforts to scramble away. The leaves rustled in anticipation. "Or no library!" Julie said quickly. Why was he afraid of the library? It was the perfect place for the mice—their friends could visit easily and discreetly, plus Linda, the children's room librarian, kept the mice safe, warm, and fed.

"She'll bring it back again!" the mouse cried. He was now framed on all sides by green. Like a wild animal, the Wild was poised to pounce. "She won't stop. She wants it back."

"Bring what back?" Julie asked. Did he mean the Wild? And what did he mean "again"? Was he talking about the person who made the wish? Did he know who was responsible for bringing the Wild back? No one had confessed yet.

Was it someone in the library? Was that why he didn't want to return there? Was it . . . It was a crazy thought, but . . . Could it have been a librarian? Three blind mice might not have noticed the presence of a quiet librarian after hours. They could have sung or talked. A librarian could have overheard something she shouldn't have. "Did the children's room librarian make the wish that set the Wild free?" Julie asked.

"Linda?" Mom said, startled. "Not Linda."

"You know!" the mouse shrieked.

It *was* Linda! Oh, wow, how was that possible? Linda? Smiley, friendly, ordinary Linda? She made the wish that set the Wild free? She was responsible for Julie nearly losing her family, her home, everything? But how—

"She'll know you know!" He stumbled backward, and his hind paws touched the green. Instantly, the vines snapped around him. Leaves fanned over his face, and the Wild swept him under Julie's bed. He vanished in a knot of green shadows.

"No!" Julie rushed forward.

Mom grabbed her arm. "Stop! It has a character! It's going to grow!" She pulled Julie back into the hallway. "Boots! Precious! Get the pruners!" Mom spun Julie around by the shoulders and aimed her toward the stairs. "Go!"

"Only if you go," Julie said. "You go; I go. You stay; I stay." She was not—repeat, *not*—going to lose Mom to the Wild again.

Before October, Mom wouldn't have listened. But now she nodded and released Julie. Side by side, Julie and her mom stood in the bedroom doorway. Green undulated under the bed, pulsing. Julie swallowed. Her mouth felt papery dry. It could happen again—losing her family, losing herself, all of it. She couldn't let it happen again.

Julie heard *thump, thump, thump*. Dragging two pairs

of pruning shears, Boots and Precious came up the stairs. They dropped them at Julie and Mom's feet. Eyes on the Wild, Mom reached down, picked up the longer shears, and held them ready. Julie picked up the smaller clippers and snapped them open and shut.

Precious pranced into the bedroom. "I see no new growth."

"It ate the third mouse," Julie said.

"Oh. Best be going." Flicking her tail in the air, the white cat bolted out of the room and down the stairs. A few seconds later, Julie heard the cat door in the kitchen creak.

Boots hesitated. "Coming?"

Mom hefted the pruners. "We have to try to cut it back as soon as it grows. Once it grows too much, it will be too strong to stop."

Boots inched backward. "Since there are only two pruners and only two people with opposable thumbs . . ."

"You can go," Mom said.

Boots fled, a streak of orange fur.

A minute passed, and then another and another. Julie's arms began to ache from holding the pruners. Her palms sweated on the handles until they felt slick.

"What's it doing?" Julie asked.

Mom shook her head. "I don't know. It's had enough time to force the mouse into a fairy tale. It should be growing by now."

They watched deep green shadows writhe under Julie's bed in a mass of tentacle-like vines. She heard the *shush-shush* of leaves rubbing together. But it didn't grow. Why not? What was it doing? "Let him go!" Julie shouted at the green. "Give him back!"

The Wild burst out from under the bed. Julie's heart slammed against her rib cage. Oh, no, oh, no. She gripped the shears as leaves and vines spilled across the carpet—

And then just as suddenly, the green retreated. In its wake, it left behind a huddled lump of red and blue velvet.

The velvet moaned. Julie saw hands reach out of the fabric to press against the rug. The figure pushed upward to kneel in the center of Julie's carpet. He raised his head.

Beside her, Julie heard her mom suck in a breath. The pruning shears slipped from Mom's fingers and clattered to the floor.

"Rapunzel," the man said.

"Dad," Julie said.

## Chapter Two
### *Rapunzel's Prince*

One minute.

Two minutes.

Julie felt the word *dad* still vibrating on her lips. Beside her, Mom was an ice sculpture. Color ran out of her perpetually rosy cheeks as Julie's father, Rapunzel's prince, slowly pushed himself onto his feet and straightened.

Julie felt herself pale, then flush, then pale again. Dad!

He looked exactly as Julie remembered from her single afternoon with him: sandy tousled hair, Superman cleft chin, blue eyes that matched Mom's, and pale scars etched on his cheeks from the thorns at the base of Rapunzel's tower . . . How did he look to Mom? She had last seen him five centuries ago, when he'd sacrificed himself so that she and the other fairy-tale characters could escape the Wild.

Five centuries.

If Mom were anyone else, she would have fainted dead

away. But she was Rapunzel, and Rapunzel did not faint. She handled every situation with grace and style . . . Okay, every situation except this one. Mom didn't move or speak. She simply stood there, pale and silent.

Julie felt as if there wasn't enough oxygen in the room. It was hard to breathe. She felt dizzy, light-headed. She saw Dad's eyes flick around the room at the movie posters, the strewn clothes, the floppy-eared teddy bear on the dresser, the jeans hanging from the closet doorknob, and—behind him—the tangled mass of leaves and vines that was the Wild, half hidden in the shadows under her bed. His eyes raised back up, first to Rapunzel and then to Julie.

Julie laughed out loud. She couldn't help it—the laugh just burst out of her as wild and shrill as a scream. Her dad was here! Here, here, here! She leapt over a stack of over-due library books, landed in a heap of sweaters, and then slammed into her father. She threw her arms around his neck. "You're here! How are you here? You're free!"

His arms closed around her as if by reflex. She pressed her cheek against silk and velvet and breathed him in. He was real! He was here! He smelled exactly as she remembered: like pine sap and ancient dust. Tears in her eyes, she tilted her head up to see his face. He wasn't looking at her. Why wasn't he looking at her? He was staring over Julie's head at Mom. Oh, of course, she thought.

Releasing him, she wiped her eyes with the back of her

hand and then tugged on his silk sleeve. "Come on. Say hello to your true love." Her voice cracked on the last word. She led him across the room to the doorway where Mom stood, frozen.

Mom lifted her hand halfway toward him, and then her hand fell back down. Julie had never seen her look so pale. She was as ghostly as a reflection in a window. "You're not dreaming, Mom," Julie said. "He's real. See, here." She grabbed his hand and Mom's hand, and she put them together.

Their fingers intertwined.

Julie stepped back. Wow. She stared at her parents' hands, their fingers laced together for the first time in five hundred years. Mom's fingers were thin and smooth, with nails tapered in half-crescent moons. Dad's fingers were calloused and brown, and he had soft, pale hair across the veins on the back of his hand. Julie looked up at her parents' faces. Both of them were staring at their hands.

"Rapunzel," Dad said, more a breath than a sound. "My Zel."

Mom raised her face, and Julie saw her eyes glisten. But she didn't cry. She wouldn't cry, Julie knew. In Mom's original story, Rapunzel cried when she was reunited with her prince. Her tears were the final moment of her story. In the Wild, that meant that once she cried, she would forget who she was, and she would be caught in an endless cycle of reenacting the same tale over and over again. After living through that, Mom wasn't going to cry now.

Dad was crying. Tears zigzagged down his scars. Slowly, gently, Zel reached up and touched the tears with her fingertips. Lightly, she brushed them away.

And now her parents were inches away from each other. Julie hadn't seen them move. Only their hands touched. Zel's free hand hovered by her prince's face, almost but not quite touching. In each of their eyes, Julie could see the reflection of the other, filling the blue. Their breathing fell into unison, exhales mingling in the space between their lips.

Julie felt as if a bubble had closed around them, and she was outside looking in. But that's okay, she told herself. They deserve a moment. I should leave them alone.

She didn't move. She couldn't move. She couldn't stop staring at them. Her parents were together!

"You're here," Mom said.

"Yes," Dad said.

Again, silence. Mom traced the curve of Dad's cheek with her fingers. He ran his hand through her wheat gold hair. "You are free," Dad said.

"Yes," Mom said.

Silence.

"Whoa!" a voice said from the hallway. Julie looked down. Fur on end, Boots lashed his tail from side to side. "What the . . . How's this . . ." Rising onto his hind feet, he pointed at Dad with his front paw. "You are so not a mouse."

Dad inclined his head. "Puss-in-Boots. It is good to see you."

Bending, Julie scooped up her brother. "Come on. Let them say hello in peace." She carted him out of the room and down the stairs.

He squirmed in her arms, shedding orange fur on her shirt. "Just for the record: I didn't abandon you," he said. "I had to be sure that Precious was safe, and then I was coming back to fight alongside you."

Uh-huh. "You were curious," Julie said, carrying him into the kitchen. "You didn't see the Wild take over the house so you came to see why not."

"That too," Boots said. With a final twist, he wiggled out of her arms and landed on the kitchen table. "Now, explain the whole miracle-escape thing to me."

It *was* a miracle. A bona fide, inexplicable miracle. She remembered the moment she last saw Dad: in front of room thirteen, a motel room door in the middle of a castle. It had led magically to the Wishing Well Motel, where she had made the wish that had banished the Wild back under her bed. She had chosen to walk through that door and make that wish. She had never expected to see him again. "I can't explain it," she said. "The mouse ran in, and Dad came out."

He licked his fur back flat. "That is the most unsatisfying explanation I've ever heard," he said. "Did he say how he escaped? Did the mouse rescue him? Was it more like a hostage exchange?"

"Maybe," Julie said. "I don't know. We didn't ask."

"Your dad suddenly appears after being imprisoned for five hundred years, and you don't ask? I know you're not a cat, but do you have zero curiosity? Don't you wonder what this means?" He leapt off the table and wound around chair legs—the cat equivalent of pacing—and continued with questions: Did this mean that the Wild was weakening? Was this a white flag of surrender, or was it part of some elaborate plot? Had the Wild felt pity, or had the prince escaped on his own? Was it an accident? The Wild had never released anyone willingly before. Why now?

Good questions. But Julie had another one: What would it be like to have a dad? She tried out the word: *dad*. This is my dad. This weekend, my dad and I . . . what? What would they do now that he was here? Anything. Everything.

"Yoo-hoo, Julie. Talking here," Boots said.

Julie focused on her brother. "Sorry. What?"

He sighed theatrically. "Never mind. You'd better call your grandmother. You're lucky that Zel talked her out of her trip to Europe. She'll want to know what happened. Maybe she'll know why it happened."

Right. Yes. "And I should call Gillian. She'll never believe this."

"She hangs out with a dancing bear," Boots said. "You could tell her that Santa Claus is your roomie, and she'd believe you."

"Point taken," Julie said, and smiled. Once she started smiling, she couldn't stop. She felt like her innards were about to burst out, like her skin was too small to hold in all the shouting and jumping inside her. Dad, Dad, Dad! How many times had she imagined him here? A million times. A billion. She wanted to race back upstairs and see if he was still here. But no, Mom deserved a moment with Dad. Julie had waited twelve years, but Mom had waited five hundred. On the other hand, he was Julie's dad, and she'd only met him once—and then chosen to leave him in the Wild. Her smile faded. Did he understand why she'd done it? Did he blame her?

"Okay, Attention Deficit Girl, you just ignore me," Boots said. "I'm going to tell Precious it's safe." As he squeezed his bulk out the cat door, he said over his shoulder, "By the way, the mice are in the fridge."

*That* caught Julie's attention. She sprang across the kitchen. What was he thinking? Mice in the fridge? She threw open the refrigerator door.

Two tail-less, shivering mice fell out into her hands.

"So cold," one said. "So very, very cold."

"Winter, winter, go away, come again another day," the second one said.

She winced. "I'm so sorry." Kicking the fridge door shut, she cupped the mice in her hands and carried them to the counter. She needed a box in case they freaked out again. She fetched the shoe box from her new sneakers out of the trash, wrapped the mice in a dish towel, and laid them in the box. "Better?" she asked.

"Thank you, kind maid!" one of them sang.

She made a face. They weren't going to think she was so kind when they heard what had happened. She might have gained a father, but they'd lost a brother. Who knew how long he'd be trapped in the Wild? It had kept Rapunzel's prince for five hundred years.

Julie's eyes shifted toward the ceiling. Wow, Dad was here.

Was she a bad person for not feeling worse? Honestly, if she had known that all it would take to have her family together would be one talking mouse, she would have chucked all three rodents in years ago. Ugh, did that make her a horrible person? Taking a deep breath, she told them the news as quickly as she could. The two mice began to sob. "I'm so sorry," she repeated. "We'll take you two someplace safe . . ." She trailed off. They'd promised to take the third mouse home to his nice, safe cage in the library . . .

She'd nearly forgotten: Linda had made the wish! *Linda.*

Perky, cheerful Linda, the children's room librarian who always remembered every kid's name and had been known to skip around the library singing when new books arrived. She always seemed so harmless, so . . . librarian-like. How could she have been the one who had turned Julie's world upside down? It was crazy, nearly as crazy as Dad returning. Why had Linda done it? What did she want? Did she know what would happen when she made her wish? Did she know her wish would come true?

Gently, Julie closed the lid on the shoe box. The mice murmured to each other, whimpering and moaning. Once they recovered, Julie could ask them more about the librarian. How much of the truth did Linda know? Did she know about Julie's family? Did she know that Mom was the original Rapunzel and that she had defeated the Wild at the end of the Middle Ages? Or, more accurately, that she and Dad had defeated the Wild, though it had cost Dad his freedom . . .

Julie heard footsteps on the stairs. Clutching the box of mice, she ran out of the kitchen and through the living room. Mom appeared at the top of the stairs. Where was Dad? Was he still here? Had the Wild recaptured him? "Is Dad . . ."

"Julie," Mom said. She was smiling so brightly that she seemed to gleam. She skipped down the stairs two at a time and then wrapped her arms around Julie. The box with the mice tumbled out of Julie's hands.

The box landed upside down. Hugging Mom, Julie placed her foot lightly on the box, holding it down. Over Mom's shoulder, Julie saw Dad walk down the stairs. His hand rested on his sword hilt to keep the sword from batting against the steps. He was smiling so broadly that his scars disappeared into his cheeks.

And her mother, the unflappable Rapunzel, cried into Julie's shoulder.

## Chapter Three
### *The Wicked Witch*

In the garage, the prince circled the car once, twice, three times.

"Think of it like a pumpkin coach," Julie said, "but with invisible horses." Fidgeting, she shot a look at the door to the kitchen and wished Mom would hurry up. Mom had called the Wishing Well Motel to warn Grandma that they were on their way. Once the initial shock had worn off, Mom had begun to raise all the same questions that Boots had asked. Dad hadn't known any of the answers. So they were off to see Grandma. Maybe she knew what it meant that the Wild had released Dad. Smart idea, but if Mom stayed on the phone any longer, Julie was going to have to explain the internal combustion engine. And, really, the rest of the world. Where did she even begin? He'd missed so much. She opened the front passenger-side car door. "You can sit here if you want. Mom will be out soon." She hoped.

It was so hard to know what to say to him. She wanted to say everything at once. I missed you. I'm sorry I left you. Hello, I'm your daughter. Welcome home.

Cautiously, Dad climbed in. His sword banged against the door. Contorting himself, he negotiated the point beneath the glove compartment. Volkswagens weren't designed for broadswords. I should complain to the manufacturer, she thought. Next year's model: suitable for heroic jaunts to dragons' lairs or Wal-Marts. She nearly laughed out loud, but what if he thought she was laughing at him? Julie pointed to the seat belt. "See this? You pull it across you and put the silver part into that slot." He pulled the seat belt out and then released it. It snapped back. "Pull it across you," she said. This time, he stretched it across himself and successfully buckled it. "Good. You push the red button to—"

He pushed the red button. The seat belt popped out. He grinned at her and rebuckled it. "It is a harness, is it not?" he said. "Like when one rides a dragon."

She grinned back at him. "Exactly," she said, climbing into the backseat. Okay, maybe this wouldn't be too hard. All she had to do to explain modern technology was relate it to dragons and unicorns and fairy godmothers.

Hurrying into the garage, Mom said, "Oh, you're ready. Good." She hit the automatic garage door opener, and the door rattled as it rolled up.

The prince grabbed for his sword hilt and tried to stand. The seat belt locked into position, and the sword whacked the car door. "It's okay!" Julie shouted. "Just a door! A magic door!"

He settled down.

Mom slid into the driver's seat and handed the shoe box with the two blind mice to Julie. "Did Julie tell you where we're going?" Mom asked Dad.

Ahh, she hadn't exactly gotten that far yet. Explaining the lawn mower, the beach chairs, and Gillian's dancing bear had distracted them. "We're going to Grandma's motel," Julie said. She wondered if this was going to be a problem. In their fairy tale, Dad and Grandma weren't exactly friends. "You knew her as Dame Gothel, Rapunzel's witch. But don't worry—she's not evil anymore."

The prince was about to respond, but then Mom put the car in reverse and backed out of the garage. Dad clutched the sides of his seat. Julie couldn't help smiling. What was it like to see the world for the first time?

Julie's father leaned against the window with his palm pressed to the glass as they drove across town. All the streets were still damaged from their time as part of a fairy-tale forest. Potholes pockmarked the road, and telephone poles were askew. Dad had no way of knowing this wasn't normal, Julie thought. It must all look equally strange to him. They passed Bigelow Nurseries, which had only recently reopened. The Wild had caused all of its flowers and other plants to sprout and spread, and it had taken a while to clear away the excess growth. Agway was missing its giant rooster sign, which had transformed into a witch's house on chicken legs and wandered across town. It of course became inanimate again as soon as the Wild was defeated, but the sign was now stranded several miles from the store. Dunkin' Donuts had a new drive-though to replace the one that had been destroyed by a fast-growing magic bean-stalk . . . Julie's wish in the well might have restored her life to normal, but it hadn't turned back the clock or erased any consequences. The aftereffects of the Wild continued to linger. Glass slippers, poisoned apples, and spinning wheels littered the town. Gingerbread houses moldered in the open air. Spells and enchantments continued to cause otherwise ordinary people to catch flies with their tongues or dance until midnight.

Mom slowed to a stop at a traffic light. Julie expected her to point out her beauty parlor, Rapunzel's Hair Salon, which was across the street, next to CVS. But she just kept staring up at the light until it changed. Maybe Mom didn't know what to say. Julie tried to imagine what this must be like for her. To Julie, it felt like looking at a sunset and then realizing the fire is actually a phoenix. Or like looking at steam from a manhole cover and knowing it's really dragon smoke. Or like looking at the moon and imagining astronauts walking on it. It was both so utterly impossible and absolutely real at the same time. He was a dream that had walked out of their heads into daylight. Julie didn't want to stop looking at him. If she did, he might vanish back into dreams again.

As Mom turned into the parking lot of the Wishing Well Motel, Julie saw how hard she was clutching the steering wheel.

"Mom, are you okay?" Julie asked.

"Let's get inside," Mom said, "before anyone sees us." She parked and left the car. As if standing guard, she surveyed the mostly empty parking lot.

The prince unlatched his seat belt and then stared at the door. He ran his hands over the upholstery and the lock/unlock buttons. Pulling on her coat, Julie hopped out and opened the car door for him. "Thank you," he said. Standing, he regarded the motel as Julie fetched the box of mice from the backseat. "This is where the wicked witch lives now?"

The Wishing Well Motel had never been a five-star resort. To be completely honest, the best adjective to describe the twenty-room motel was "dumpy." Teal and orange paint peeled like a sunburn. The sidewalk was fractured into concrete flagstones. The only feature less than thirty years old was the brand-new barbed wire fence that corralled the wishing well in the backyard. But still, Julie loved this place. She'd spent countless weekends and summers here. She opened her mouth to defend it, but before she could reply, the lobby door flew open. Bells jangled from the top of the door, and Grandma filled the doorway. Instantly, Dad's hand clamped onto his sword hilt. Julie squeezed his other hand. "Not evil," she reminded him.

He shot a tight smile at her. "Habit."

"Bad habit," she said.

"For you, I will endeavor to break it."

She blushed, not sure how to respond. That sounded so . . . princely.

Grandma shooed them inside. "Quickly, quickly!" She slammed the door shut behind them, flipped the sign to Closed, and yanked the shades down. Without taking her eyes off Grandma, Julie hung her coat next to Mom's on the coatrack. Grandma was flushed, and her frizzed white hair danced around her head as if electrically charged.

What was wrong? Julie wondered. She looked from Grandma to Mom and back to Grandma and felt as if she were missing something. Why was Grandma upset? Everything was great now. Dad was here! He was free!

Grandma's housedress billowed out like a cape as she spun around to face them. Julie saw her take a deep, steadying breath. "You look . . . the same," she said to the prince.

He bowed slightly. Julie noticed that his hand still

hovered near his sword hilt. He didn't touch it, though. Point to Dad. "You look . . . less evil," he said.

"It's the flowers," Grandma said, gesturing at her dress. "You can't look evil in a floral print. Stripes, maybe. Polka dots, definitely. But not flowers. Why are you here?"

"Identification," Mom said. She began to pace between the puke green pleather couches. "I told you on the phone. He needs a driver's license, birth certificate, social security number . . ."

Julie hadn't thought about all that. Guess there were a few complications associated with a person popping out of nowhere. Who knew that miracles came with paperwork problems?

Grandma waved Mom's words away. Her eyes were fixed on Dad. She had, Julie noticed, not put in her tinted contact lenses. Without them, her natural eye color was red. It was like watching a mink size up its prey. "Why are you here in this world?"

"Why are you?" he countered. Julie saw his hand wrap around his sword hilt. "You should have been defeated. Rapunzel should be free. Yet here she comes to you. What power do you still wield?"

Whoa! Maybe they should have briefed him a little more thoroughly on the drive here. "*Not* evil, remember?" Julie whispered to Dad.

Red eyes piercing, Grandma circled Dad. "You have your

vision, but you also have **the thorn** scars. You do not remember how you escaped?"

"I do not," he said.

"Why would it release you?" Grandma demanded. "It should be forcing you to complete scenes from fairy tales."

No fighting! This was supposed to be a happy reunion! Julie tried to step between Dad and Grandma and instead bumped into a coffee table. Decades-old magazines spilled onto the floor. "Maybe it was a trade," she said. Reaching across the coffee table, Julie held the shoe box with the two mice out toward Grandma. "The Wild has the third mouse now. It didn't lose anything by releasing the prince." Honestly, it sounded like Grandma was blaming Dad— like his return was something suspicious, not something wonderful!

"It should have kept both you *and* the mouse. It should have used the opportunity to grow. The Wild *always* wants to grow." Grandma shook her head. "I don't understand this, and I don't trust this. After hundreds of years, the Wild doesn't simply turn *nice*." She glared at all of them, as if this mystery were their fault.

"Yet I am meant to believe that you did," the prince said.

True, but Grandma had turned nice over several centuries. As of a few weeks ago, the Wild had wanted to take over the world. Julie knew that firsthand—she was, in fact, the only person she knew who had ever talked to the Wild directly—and could vouch that it wasn't likely to turn nice anytime soon. The Wild had (briefly) possessed her brother Boots and spoken to her through him, as if he were a puppet. "Maybe Dad's escape was an accident," Julie said. "Or maybe . . ." What were the other theories Boots had mentioned? She hadn't really been listening. "Maybe Dad did pull off an escape and just doesn't remember how."

"All possible," Mom said. She shot a smile at Julie. Julie could tell that she meant it to be a reassuring smile, but she just looked worried. "We can debate the cause later. Right now, we need to take care of the immediate danger—"

*Crash.* Julie jumped as the lobby door was flung open. Dad drew his sword. Steel rang like a bell against the scabbard. Grandma crouched, hands ready to cast a spell. Mom thrust the shoe box onto a couch, shielding the mice.

Cinderella's fairy godmother, one of the motel guests, bustled through the door. "Snow's seven need help! Rose's thorns are out of control—Oh, my, it's you! You're out!" She bounded across the lobby and threw her arms around Dad's neck. As she hugged him, she hopped up and down. Her beach-bag-sized purse knocked against her, and her cloak slipped off her shoulders, exposing fairy wings that fluttered as she bounced. "I can't believe it! You're here!"

Dad held the sword behind him, careful not to hurt the bouncing fairy.

"Do you remember me?" she asked, releasing him. She twirled in a circle and mimed tapping him with a wand. "Poof! You're a pumpkin! Does that ring a bell?"

He resheathed his sword and bowed. "Of course I remember you, Lady Fairy. It is an honor to see you again. Did you say someone is in distress?"

The fairy godmother giggled. "'Lady Fairy.' I haven't been called that in ages. You can call me Bobbi." She waggled her eyebrows. "You can call me anytime." She poked Zel. "You lucky, lucky ducky! What an unexpected treat!"

"Exactly. Unexpected," Mom said. "We need to make him real before anyone official notices his existence. It's not a good time to simply appear." Julie had never seen Mom look so worried. Lines creased her forehead. On anyone else, this would have been ordinary. On Mom, who (like the other fairy-tale characters) didn't age, the wrinkles stood out stark on her pale forehead.

"Am I not real?" Dad said.

"We need to set him up with identification," Mom continued. "And a history. We can't let anyone know he came from the Wild." Mom was right, Julie thought. A lot of people were on the lookout for strange things like a man suddenly springing into existence. Reporters and scientists had practically taken over the town. Northboro even had some bona fide tourists. If anyone decided to question Dad . . . Julie shivered. There was so much he didn't know.

He'd give away their secret in seconds. She was beginning to understand why Mom looked so stressed.

Dad frowned. "Why can no one know that I am from the Wild? It is the truth."

"My dears, look no further! Help is here!" Bobbi said. She rooted through her purse. "Now, where did I put . . . Aha! Here it is!" She drew out a wand. Sparkles dripped off the tip of it like a Fourth of July sparkler. She waved it at the prince. "Bibbity—"

"Do not humiliate yourself with that phrase," Grandma said.

"Oh, pooh, you're no fun." She stuck out her tongue at Grandma. Spinning toward the prince, she tapped him with the wand.

Sparkles swirled around his body like a hundred fireflies, spiraling up to his hair and down around his feet. In an instant, he was bathed in glittery light. He held up his hand, studying it as the sparks darted around his fingers.

Bobbi giggled and bounced up and down.

When the glitter faded, Julie's dad looked . . . normal. He wore khakis, a white oxford shirt, brown shoes, and a brown belt. Even his hair was trimmed and tamed. He reached for his hip. "My sword!"

"You silly," Bobbi said. "You don't need that here. This is the suburbs."

"You stand out too much with it," Mom said. She

then turned to Grandma. "Next, we need proof of identification . . ."

Softly, Dad said, "No."

Mom frowned, a delicate crease appearing between her eyebrows. Julie knew that look: Mom was struggling to keep her temper. Please, Julie thought, don't fight with Dad. He just came back. He's new here. He doesn't know anything. He didn't know what a driver's license was. He hadn't even known what a car was.

A little louder, Dad said, "I am in a world I have never seen, five hundred years from anything I know. I come with you in your horseless coach to this witch's lair and let spells be cast upon me. I do this because I trust you, because you are my love, and because you are here with my flesh and blood. But do not ask me to go defenseless into this new world. Do not ask this of me."

For the second time since Dad's return, Julie saw her mother's eyes glisten with tears. Mom was, she realized, close to breaking. Dad's return—it wasn't anything she was prepared for. Ever. Mom didn't know what to do. And she was scared. But Dad was placing enormous trust in them, and they were stripping him of everything familiar. "Mom," Julie said. Her voice cracked. She cleared her throat and tried again. "Maybe . . . maybe he could disguise it somehow?"

Eyes still over-bright, Mom continued to stare at Dad, though she spoke to Grandma, "Do you have a duffel bag?

He can carry the sword in that, and it won't look so conspicuous."

"Thank you," the prince said, and bowed.

"Don't bow to me," Mom said. "Please." She reached out to touch him, but then she let her hand fall a few inches from his face.

For a long minute, no one spoke.

Julie wished they could rewind. Everything was so perfect in that moment when Dad had stood there in her room. Why couldn't it have stayed exactly like that? Why couldn't they just be together and be happy? Why did they have to be afraid of things that hadn't happened yet and might never happen? People might never even notice Dad. He might blend in fine. Or all the police and scientists and government officials could lose interest in Northboro and leave, and then everything would go back to normal . . . *better* than normal.

"Next we need a new identity for him," Grandma said.

Still only addressing his Rapunzel, Dad asked, "Why can I not be myself? It was enough for you before."

Mom's mouth formed a small *o*. She swallowed visibly.

Julie had to say something. She couldn't let this continue. "It's not you," she said to Dad. "It's just that the world doesn't know fairy-tale characters are real. We have to keep it secret."

Eyes not leaving Mom, he reached out and took Mom's

hand in his. His hands swallowed hers. "You fought for freedom. How is it freedom to hide who you are? You are out of the Wild. You should not have to play a role anymore."

Mom dropped her gaze. "It's . . . complicated," she said.

Julie winced. What was wrong with them? This was just getting worse and worse. She wanted to shake them both. True love, remember? You were apart, and now you're together! Play nice!

The prince released her hand. "Try small words and perhaps I will understand."

From the shoe box, the mice shouted, "Danger, danger!"

"Small enough for you?" Grandma asked. Her frizzed hair seemed to sizzle. "We must pretend we're the same as everyone else. People fear what's different, and ordinary people outnumber us by the billions. I will *not* play those odds with my daughter and granddaughter's safety!" Ouch—the implication was clear: Dad would endanger them. Julie wanted to protest, It's not like Dad meant to put us in danger! But Grandma wasn't finished. "All you do, all you've ever done, is complicate our lives. Ruin our happiness! Zel and I were happy in our tower until you came and stole her heart from me. I will not let you steal my happiness again!"

"Mother!" Zel said.

Abruptly, Gothel spun away. Julie saw her shoulders shaking. Oh, wow, was she *crying*? Grandma, the former wicked witch . . . No, she was shaking in anger. Wasn't she?

Leaning over the green pleather couch, Bobbi poked the shoe box with her wand. "Why do you have a talking box?" she asked, breaking the awful silence.

Mom pounced on the shoe box, clearly eager to change the subject. "It's the two blind mice." She handed the box to the fairy godmother. "Would you look after them? You have experience with mice."

"Of course, the poor dears." Lifting the lid, Bobbi clucked at them. "Don't you worry your pretty furry heads." She emptied the box into her enormous purse, and the mice squeaked as they tumbled in.

"He will need a name," Grandma said, her back still to them but her voice calm.

"Julie has already selected a name for me," the prince said, his voice soft now too. She had? Julie didn't remember doing that. She ran back through her memory of their conversations. Had they talked about names? "She calls me 'Dad.'"

Julie smiled.

Not charmed, Grandma snorted. "Mortimer? Ebenezer? Bubba?"

Tentatively, Mom said to Dad, "You have a chance to invent yourself anew, to be more than the sum of your stories. It's a marvelous opportunity." She put a world of appeal into her eyes. Julie could read it as clearly as if Mom had said out loud: *please.*

"You do not wish me to be myself," he said. "But it is this self who came to you in your tower, this self who embraced your dream of freedom, this self who fought and sacrificed for you against the Wild, this self who loves you." He touched her silken hair.

Julie felt her own eyes fill with tears. Swallowing, she spoke up: "Can't we just call him Prince? Like the rock star."

Mom nodded wordlessly as he twined his fingers through her hair.

Grandma bustled behind the registration desk. Opening cabinets, she pulled out papers, pens, jars of crickets and eyeball-like grapes (or were they grape-like eyeballs? Julie knew better than to ask). She scooted aside a bowl of apples, and Bobbi plucked a MacIntosh from the top. She tossed it into the air.

"I will not disguise my origins," Prince said. "I am not ashamed of my past, and I will not hide who I am out of mere fear. I am the prince. I rescue damsels in distress—"

Bobbi caught the apple mid-air. "Oh my goodness, the dwarves! The thorns! I forgot about Sleeping Beauty!"

Dad paled. "A princess is in danger while we linger here?"

"She's not in danger," Mom said. "She's perfectly safe,

asleep and hidden in one of the motel rooms. We'll find a way to wake her soon." Rose might be safe, Julie thought, but she was not going to be happy when she woke. Julie had heard that she never slept more than an hour at a time for fear of never waking up. When Rose discovered that she'd been trapped in her story again . . . Sleeping Beauty had one of the worst fairy tales of any heroine. She was exiled from her family at birth, lied to about her identity by the people who raised her, and then forced to spend the rest of her story comatose. Julie shuddered.

"She fell asleep in the Wild, and no one woke her before the Wild was defeated," Bobbi explained to Dad. "But that's not really the problem. The problem is the thorns. They won't stop growing. In her fairy tale, they're supposed to grow into a barrier around her, but now that she's out of the Wild . . ." Shrugging expressively, Bobbi tossed the apple from hand to hand. "Snow's seven are here to keep the thorns at bay—and because of their experience with guarding inert women."

"Why does her prince not wake her?" Dad asked. His hand, Julie noticed, was on his sword hilt again. If there were a white stallion nearby, she bet he would be leaping on it right about now.

"He said no," Bobbi said. "He said he's 'moved on.'" Julie knew from Mom that that wasn't all he'd said. He'd also said that he wouldn't be responsible for making the Wild grow—fairy-tale moments enacted by real fairy-tale characters fueled the Wild an incredible amount even when they happened *outside* the Wild.

"I am a prince," Dad said. "I will wake her!" Spinning on his heels, he strode out of the lobby. The bells on the door jangled.

"Wait!" Mom cried. She rushed out the door after Dad.

"I told you," Grandma said. "He's trouble." Dropping her magical supplies, she stalked around the registration desk. Hurrying after Gothel, Bobbi shook her back until her wings lay flat, and then she rewrapped her cloak around her shoulders. Under it, her wings looked like an ordinary bulge due to bad posture or old age.

Outside, Julie spotted Sleeping Beauty's motel room instantly. Thick brambles spilled out the window of room twenty-three and snaked up the door to encase the doorknob. A knot of thorns twisted over the rusted air conditioner.

"Oops," Bobbi said.

Julie's heart started to thud faster. It's not the Wild, she told herself. These brambles were brown. The Wild was a bright, lush summer green. But the growing thorns looked enough like the Wild that she felt her palms begin to sweat.

"This is *not* good," Mom said. "Someone might see this!" She shot a look at the parking lot. Beyond the Vacancy sign, Julie saw cars whiz by on Main Street. So far, no one had noticed, but if the thorns grew much more . . . The last thing they needed was to draw attention to the Wishing Well Motel, the site of the magic wishing well.

"Why didn't you say something?" Gothel growled at Bobbi, who was again tossing the apple from hand to hand.

She caught the apple. "Hmm? Oh, I got distracted." She waved a hand at Prince, who was poking at the brambles around the doorknob.

"Do you have any gardening shears or . . ." Mom began to ask.

Dad drew his sword out of the duffel bag. "Prince, no!" Mom said. He swung at the doorknob. Brambles shriveled away from the sword, retreating from the door. Mom ran forward and grabbed his arm. "Stop!" she shouted. "You can't behave like you're in a fairy tale! You'll make the Wild grow! Please, Prince. Fairy-tale actions by real fairy-tale characters fuel the Wild more than anything else!"

But it was too late. He was through the thorn barrier. He reached down with his free hand, twisted the doorknob, and pushed the door open.

Had Dad fueled the Wild? How much had it grown? Had Julie lost her room? Her house? No, it couldn't have grown that much. He'd only swung his sword a couple of times, and it was only a small patch of brambles. At worst, the

Wild had expanded a few feet beyond her bed. They could easily trim it back.

All of them quickly piled into the motel room. Grandma switched on the fluorescent bulb. Sickly green light flickered on, illuminating the peeling beige wallpaper and the well-worn orange shag carpet. A two-decade-old TV set perched on the chipped dresser. Faded photographs of Worcester landmarks decorated the wall. And Snow White's seven dwarves lay curled up on the floor, sound asleep, axes beside them. They'd been caught inside the thorns' spell. Seven voices snored in unison.

In the center of the room, Julie saw a queen-sized bed with a tacky brown and green 1970s bedspread. In the bed lay a beautiful blonde woman. Her lips were slightly parted, as if waiting for a kiss. She was the only one not snoring. Dad strode toward her. Grandma planted herself firmly between Dad and Sleeping Beauty. Red eyes flashing, she put her hands on her hips. "Let me pass, witch," he said.

Mom clung to his arm. "No, you can't!" she said.

Julie ran forward and grabbed Dad's other arm. "Please, Dad! You'll make the Wild grow! Listen to Mom!"

"You will not let me save her?" Dad asked, confusion filling his face. "But I am still a hero even here in this strange world, am I not?"

From the doorway, Bobbi the fairy godmother said, "We shall see." She tossed the apple out the door, and she waved her wand at it. Sparkles flew, and the apple instantly ballooned. Tiny buds sprouted and grew into wheels. The peel split and rolled back to create windows and a door.

"What are you *doing*?!" Gothel began to step away from the bed and then halted, eyes fixing back on Prince. "Don't you move an inch." She shook her finger at him.

Bobbi reached into her oversized purse, drew out the two blind mice, and wiggled her wand at them. Growing, they leapt out of her hands. Their paws hit the ground with the clatter of hooves as they changed into two white horses.

Releasing Prince, Zel rushed toward her. "Stop! You'll draw *more* attention—"

The fairy godmother smiled. "Sorry, but I don't take orders from you anymore, Zel. But thank you for bringing the prince here." What was she talking about? What did she mean, "thank you"? She waved her wand again, this time directly at Mom.

Sparkles descended over her. With a pop, Mom shrank, zooming down toward the carpet. In an instant, an orange pumpkin sat on the floor. Julie screamed. "Mom!" She threw herself onto her knees beside the pumpkin.

"You—" Grandma began.

Quickly, Bobbi flashed her wand toward Gothel. In an instant, a second pumpkin lay on the motel room floor. "No! Grandma!" Julie cried. As Bobbi waved her wand for a third and final time, Julie dove down behind a sleeping dwarf.

But the sparkles weren't aimed at Julie.

In a halo of golden glitter, the body of Sleeping Beauty

rose into the air and sailed out of the motel room, over the two pumpkins and seven sleeping dwarves, and into the open door of the apple carriage. "There's a damsel in distress," Bobbi said to Dad. "If you're truly a hero, you'll come save her." She tapped herself on the head with her wand and vanished.

An instant later, the apple coach (drawn by two blind and tail-less horses and driven by the fairy godmother) dashed out of the parking lot in a clatter of hooves. Dad ran out of the motel room. Julie sprang to her feet. "Wait! Mom and Grandma—" Julie shouted, chasing after him.

Dad raced to Mom's car. He pulled on the door handles. It didn't open; Mom had locked it. "Where are you going?" Julie called. "They're pumpkins!" She pointed back toward the motel room, where the two pumpkins lay. "She turned Mom—your love!—into a pumpkin!"

"She will be caught and punished!" he said as he ran to the motel lobby and flung open the door. He reappeared a second later with one of Grandma's brooms in his hand.

"Dad, stop!" Julie cried. What was he doing? She raced across the parking lot. As Dad jumped on the broomstick, Julie grabbed for him. She wasn't strong enough to stop him or even slow him. Wrapping her arms around his waist, Julie did the only thing she could think of: She climbed on the broomstick behind him.

He leaned forward, and they flew after the giant apple.

## Chapter Four
### The Big Apple

Up ahead, the red apple coach zigzagged down Main Street, dodging cars and veering onto the sidewalk. Car horns blared as the blind and tail-less horses thundered by, faster than any ordinary horse could run. At Rapunzel's Hair Salon, they turned right and shot down Church Street toward the highway.

Julie clung to her father's waist as they flew after the coach. "Dad, stop! We have to go back! Mom and Grandma are pumpkins!"

"Do not fear!" Dad shouted. "I will catch the villain!"

No, no, no, they had to turn around right now! Mom needed them! "Your true love is a fruit! We have to help her!" She saw the green sign for the entrance to Route 290. "Not the highway! Dad, please, turn around!"

"Rapunzel will be herself again when the clock strikes midnight," Dad said. "And I will be there to present her with her enemy! She will know then that I am still her hero!" He flew over the highway.

An eighteen-wheeler rumbled by below, and a gust of wind slammed up into Dad and Julie. Dad fought to control the broomstick, and Julie shrieked as they flipped upside down. Her coat flopped over her face. Blood rushed to her head. Above them, cars streaked by. Below them, the sky opened wide and blue.

"Lean left!" he shouted.

She leaned, and Dad jerked the handle of the broomstick sideways. They spiraled. Oh, I'm going to throw up! Julie thought. She gritted her teeth together as they spun to face the ground, the sky, the ground, the sky. . . . He wrestled the broomstick until they steadied, finally upright again.

Dad leaned forward, and the broomstick sped up. The apple coach now (impossibly) raced down the highway at twice the speed of any vehicle on the road. Looking like a spherical race car, it wove between cars and trucks as they whizzed past Boylston, Shrewsbury, and then Worcester.

"Please, please, please, stop!" she begged.

He didn't.

He yanked the broomstick to the right, and they zoomed over an exit ramp. Up ahead, she saw the apple coach zip through a tollbooth so fast that the toll collectors must have thought they'd imagined it. A few seconds later, Dad and Julie flew over the tollbooth and zoomed over the Mass Pike. At exit 9, the coach sped through another toll booth.

This was ridiculous. This was *beyond* stupid. What were they doing?

*Entering Connecticut.*

What? Did that sign just say they'd entered another *state?* "Dad, please!" How many people must have seen them between the Wishing Well Motel and here? When Mom found out they'd chased a magic coach at super-speed down multiple major highways in broad daylight . . . "We have to go back! Mom would want us to go back!"

"Rapunzel does not need me now," he said. "I can serve her best by doing what I do best: rescuing princesses."

This was a big mistake. A huge mistake. A massive misunderstanding. There had to be an explanation for why Bobbi had changed Mom and Grandma into pumpkins and taken Sleeping Beauty. There had to be a *good* explanation. "She's the fairy godmother, not a kidnapper," Julie said. "If you just turn around and help Mom change back into herself, she'll sort everything out!"

"If we stop now, we will lose the apple," Dad said. "I must restore Rapunzel's friend! I must right this wrong!" He increased their speed to that of a small plane. Below, the leafless tress blurred into a sea of brown. Houses, towns, and strip malls flashed by. Wind whooshed in Julie's ears until it sounded like a steady hum, and she shivered within her coat. But still, the apple coach outpaced them, always just at the horizon.

As the exits counted down, Julie saw the blocky silhouettes of smokestacks, construction cranes, and enormous oil tanks. Beyond them, she saw the blue of the Long Island Sound. She wished she'd stayed at the motel. If she hadn't jumped on the broomstick with Dad, maybe she could have found a way to break the pumpkin spell before midnight. At the very least, she could have made sure Mom and Grandma were safe until the clock struck twelve. She'd left them on the floor of the motel room with the door wide open.

Just before the Sound, Dad dove toward an underpass. "Watch for trolls!" Dad cried. "They live under bridges!" Trolls? What about trucks and vans and cars and SUVs and . . . Julie squeezed her eyes shut as they zipped under the bridge. She heard horns honk and smelled car exhaust. When she opened them again, they were flying west. Was he ever going to stop? Or was he just going to keep flying until they hit California? She resumed trying to convince Dad to turn around, bringing up every argument she could think of, pleading with him, even ordering him. But he ignored her.

"She heads for the pinnacles!" he shouted, interrupting her.

Pinnacles? She leaned to see around Dad.

Skyscrapers. New York City. "Dad, no!" How many zillion people would see them in Manhattan? Why wouldn't he listen? He was supposed to listen to her! He was her father!

"Hang on!" he cried as they flew into the heart of New York.

They whipped through canyons of glass and steel and concrete. Wind whistled past Julie's ears. Below, the red apple zigzagged between yellow taxicabs. Dad urged the broomstick faster.

Suddenly, the coach darted down a side street. Dad yanked on the broomstick handle, and the broom fishtailed as they turned. Julie shrieked, and the bristles slapped the corner of a brick building. But Dad merely leaned forward and shot down the street.

The apple coach was a full block ahead of them.

It turned down another street. And another. With each turn, by the time Julie and Dad rounded the corner, the apple coach was farther ahead. Impossible! It had taxis and cars and pedestrians to weave between. How could it be outdistancing them? They turned another corner in time to see the apple disappear down the next street.

"Faster!" Dad yelled to the broom as they rounded a corner and flew into the heart of Times Square. Neon bombarded them on all sides: swirls of blue and white, dancing green numbers, starbursts of silver. "Witchcraft!" he shouted as green neon cascaded in front of them. "Giants!" Dad cried as he veered around a billboard with a thirty-foot photo of a pouty-faced woman in jeans. The broomstick bucked as Dad dodged the lights and signs.

Below, horns blared. Clinging to Dad's waist, Julie looked for the apple coach. Where was it? Had it already turned down another side street? Had they lost it? Out of the corner of her eye, she thought she saw a splash of red on the street below. But in seconds, they were blocks beyond it.

Had she seen the coach? Should she tell Dad? If she didn't tell him, maybe he'd give up and go home.

Or maybe he would just keep flying forever.

"Dad!" She thumped his shoulder. "I think I saw it behind us!"

Dad yanked up on the broomstick handle, and they shot skyward, flipped upside down, and corkscrewed until they were upright again and beelining back to Times Square. It happened so quickly that Julie didn't have time to scream.

"There it is!" Dad cried.

Sailing toward the sidewalk, they slowed until they skidded to a stop on the concrete. Pedestrians scattered around them. People pointed and shouted, and cameras flashed. With each flash, Dad's arm shot up as if to deflect a blow or magic spell.

Julie jumped off the broomstick. "Hide it," she begged Dad. "Quickly."

Dad's face had drained so pale that his thorn scars stood out like fresh wounds, but he stopped warding off the camera flashes for long enough to unzip the duffel bag and stuff the broomstick inside next to his sword.

"Special effects," Julie said loudly. "We're rehearsing for a movie."

Before she finished speaking, Dad strode through the crowd as if he were passing through his own kingdom. Julie hurried after him. Could Dad even act ordinary if he wanted to? He bore as much resemblance to an ordinary person as a lion did to a house cat. Instantly, the crowd parted for him as if on instinct, perhaps because on some level, they recognized him for what he was, a fairy-tale-perfect prince. Or maybe, Julie thought, because they recognized him as the guy with the flying broomstick. Regardless, in seconds, Julie and Prince were in the center of Times Square.

Near the TKTS ticket booth, the apple coach lay on its side like a wounded animal. The red-peel door hung open, and the front wheels rotated slowly, winding down. A crowd had gathered around it. Across the median strip, a TV crew filmed the coach. In the distance, Julie heard sirens.

She didn't see Sleeping Beauty, Bobbi, or the mice-turned-horses. "They're gone," Julie said, turning to Dad. "And we really, really need to leave too."

Suddenly, the pedestrians and tourists all gasped. Julie spun back around—

The coach had vanished.

In its place, she saw a circle of empty pavement. Or not quite empty pavement: an apple, an ordinary MacIntosh apple, lay in the center of Times Square. No fairy godmother, no sleeping princess, no horse-mice. Just one lonely piece of fruit.

She heard someone in the crowd repeat what she'd said earlier: "Special effects. It's for a movie." The word *movie* traveled through the crowd. Cameras flashed, and this time Dad ignored them. With a heroically determined look on his face, he strode forward into the circle of empty pavement. All eyes turned toward him. Dozens more cameras and camera phones winked. Julie saw the TV news camera fix on him. "Dad, wait!"

He bent and picked up something. Holding it aloft, he turned back to Julie with a triumphant smile. "She has left a clue!" Julie saw sunlight glint off one of Cinderella's glass slippers.

A glass slipper? *Here?* Why would there be a stray fairy-tale item in Manhattan? New York hadn't been touched by the Wild. Okay, Sleeping Beauty had just been here, but what did a glass slipper have to do with her? It wasn't part of her tale.

A woman's voice shouted, "It's for a movie! Try on the shoe and you can be a star!" Who said that? The voice sounded familiar. Standing on tiptoes, Julie scanned the crowd looking for the speaker. Why had someone said that?

Behind her, Julie heard another woman say, "Hey, honey, I'll be your Cinderella." Laughter rippled through the crowd. People pushed forward to watch. Others continued on their way. Julie was brushed aside, and for an instant, she lost sight of Dad. She squeezed through the crowd and burst out onto the sidewalk.

In front of posters for Broadway shows, Dad knelt on one knee. Giggling, a woman in a purple overcoat kicked off her high-heeled shoe and wiggled her foot in Dad's face. Her friends egged her on.

Julie panicked. He couldn't let anyone try on the shoe! That was a fairy-tale event! "Dad, no!" she said as he slipped the glass slipper over the woman's toes.

He'd done it.

Right now, Julie realized, the Wild was growing.

The shoe only fit over half her foot. The woman's heel dangled out the back. "Just squeeze it in," the woman said, laughing. Obligingly, Dad pushed. Around her, the woman's friends laughed and applauded.

"No, no, no!" Julie shouted. She jumped forward and yanked the shoe off the woman's foot. With a cry, the woman toppled backward and landed on a pile of shopping bags. "Sorry!" Julie said, and then she threw the shoe as hard as she could. It arched through the air, glistening in the sun—and then smashed against the TKTS booth. It shattered, and shards sprayed into the crowd.

Above, birds shrieked.

Beaks and talons extended, a flock of pigeons dove to-ward Times Square. Someone yelled, and then the whole crowd was screaming and running as the birds plummeted down. Julie was shoved backward. Trying to reach Dad, she struggled against the crowd and saw the birds zero in on the woman in the purple coat. The woman swung her purse at them, and Dad drew his sword out of the duffel bag and sliced at the air over the woman's head.

The birds were behaving as if they were in the Cinder-ella story, Julie realized. Not the nice Disney version. They were acting out a scene from the original Brothers Grimm: they were trying to peck out the eyes of the "stepsister" who had tried to fake fitting into the shoe. But why? The Wild wasn't controlling them. This wasn't a fairy tale; this was real life. Why were the birds doing this? They were fueling the Wild even more!

The woman screamed.

"Run!" Julie shouted at her. "Cover your eyes and run!"

Shielding her face, the woman scrambled to her feet. Car brakes screeched and horns blared as she barreled across the intersection. The birds swarmed after her, and Julie saw the news camera swing around, tracking her. She bolted into Toys "R" Us.

The birds veered up right before impact with the door and, for an instant, they formed a black cloud against the sky. Across the street, Julie saw a kid jump out of a taxi and run toward her and her dad—the only person running *toward* them, not away.

Dad sheathed his sword. "Jack comes," he said, nodding at the figure.

Jack?

Panting, the kid waved, and Julie recognized him: Jack from the Jack and the Beanstalk fairy tale. Despite being over five hundred years old, he looked about eighteen. He had a fresh farm-boy face (shaggy blond hair that flopped into his eyes and freckles that dotted his nose), but he wore New York rebel kind of clothes (black leather coat that draped down to his ankles and dark jeans with rips at the knees). Julie saw a hint of a tattoo as he lifted his arm to wave—the green leaves of a beanstalk wound up his fore-arm. "Whoa, you're free! Saw the coach on the news and came to see if any of us were in trouble. Never expected to see you here—either of you," he said as he reached them. "Need refuge? Want to come to my place?"

Across Times Square, a police siren blared. Dad tensed and spun, hand reaching into the duffel bag for his sword.

"Yes!" Julie said to Jack. She grabbed Dad's elbow. "Come on. Please!" They followed Jack back to a taxi.

"Another car?" Dad said doubtfully.

Julie saw police working their way through the crowd, questioning all the bystanders. "We can't stay here," she said. She slid in beside Jack. Clutching his duffel bag, Dad squeezed in next to her. Julie leaned across him and pulled the door shut. The sounds of Times Square faded to a muffled buzz.

Dad twisted around to study the seat back. "Where is the harness?" He mimed a seat belt. Seat belt? He was worried about the seat belt? A woman had just been attacked by pigeons! He'd reenacted a fairy-tale scene, likely helping fuel the Wild! And all of it had been filmed!

"Seat belt's broken," Jack said cheerfully. "Just don't watch." How did he manage to sound so normal? This was a disaster!

Dad frowned. "Watch what?"

The cab jumped out into traffic, and all three of them slid to the right. Julie was squashed against Jack. His coat was soft as cloth, and it smelled like plastic—fake leather? And did she smell, um, a hint of cow manure? The driver veered around a pack of pedestrians, and Julie, Prince, and Jack all slid to the left. Within the duffel bag, the sword and broomstick thunked against the door. As they slid back to the center, Dad said, "We must rescue Sleeping Beauty . . ."

Jack waved a hand to shush him. He nodded meaningfully at the driver.

None of them spoke again as they careened through the streets of New York, but Julie's brain wouldn't quiet. The Wild was growing. The Wild *had* to be growing. One of the original fairy-tale characters had re-created a fairy-tale moment. And then the birds had done the same. Julie shuddered as she imagined the tangle of vines spilling out from her room and spreading through her house . . . There was no one home to stop it. Mom and Grandma were helpless gourds. Boots and Precious couldn't wield pruning shears. How far would the Wild grow if left unchecked? Would it swallow her house? Would it spread to her street? They had to go back! Maybe Jack could help convince Dad. As soon as they were safely in Jack's apartment, she'd tell him everything. He'd understand. He'd help.

Maybe he'd even know why all this was happening. Why was there a glass slipper in the middle of Times Square? Was Dad right that it was some sort of clue? If so, what did it mean? It had to be connected to Bobbi and the apple coach. It *couldn't* be a coincidence. Maybe Bobbi had dropped it? Maybe it had fallen out of the coach? But why would it be in the coach in the first place?

And where had the birds come from? Were they ordinary pigeons, or were they the original fairy-tale birds from Cinderella's story? And either way, what had driven them to act out a scene from a fairy tale? The Wild didn't control them here. They didn't have to attack. It didn't make sense! Nothing that had happened today made sense: Dad's return from the Wild, Bobbi's bizarre behavior, and now the birds' strange attack . . . Were they connected or a coincidence?

She wanted to ask out loud, but she didn't dare, not when the taxi driver could hear her. So she sat in silence between Dad and Jack and listened to the honks, shouts, and screeches of the city as they left Times Square, the apple, and the shattered glass slipper far behind them.

## Chapter Five
### New Yorkers

The taxi squealed up to a corner. Jack whipped out a few bills, told the driver to keep the change, and then all three of them scooted out of the cab. Julie checked out the street: no apple coach, no glass slipper, no news van, no police, no insane birds, no mob of prince-hungry women. Good. She glanced over at Dad.

He was staring up at the thirty-story apartment high-rise with an odd expression on his face. Julie had an awful thought: what if he started shouting, "Rapunzel, Rapunzel, let down your hair"? Taking his elbow, she propelled him after Jack into the apartment building, past a doorman, and straight into an open elevator. The doors slid closed, and Julie sagged against a wall. Finally, *safe*.

The elevator lurched, and Dad clutched at the walls.

"Relax," Jack said to him. "You only have five hundred years' worth of technology to get used to. Did anyone tell you that men have walked on the moon? Oh, and have you tasted microwave popcorn? *Muy delicioso.*"

Dad stared at the numbers as they lit up. "Everything is very . . ." He paused as if trying to find the polite word. The elevator jolted as it reached the eleventh floor. "Loud. Your world's magic makes a lot of noise."

Jack clapped him on the shoulder. "It's a good world, though. You're in for a treat. Tonight we're going to party until the cows come home." He winked at Julie. "Kidding. The cow's already home."

Julie couldn't manage even a polite smile. "We can't stay," she said. "We have to get home." Quickly, she told Jack everything that had happened: about the third blind mouse, Dad's return, the thorns around Sleeping Beauty, Bobbi's spell . . .

"Pumpkins?" Jack burst out laughing. He had a rich, full laugh. "Now that is the best practical joke I've heard in a long time!"

He thought it was a *joke*? Mom and Grandma were fruit! Plus Bobbi hadn't acted like it was a joke. "I don't think—" Before she could finish, the elevator door slid open, and Jack's roommate Gina (the former giantess, now a mere six feet nine inches, thanks to one of Grandma's spells) rushed forward with a cry. She lifted Prince out of the elevator into a bear hug. "We thought you were dead! This is unbelievable! Look at you! You're here! Welcome to the world!" Setting him down, she bustled him into the apartment. "Come in, come in! The cow is making lunch. Do you mind vegetarian?"

She hadn't said hello to Julie or even so much as glanced at her. Feeling invisible, Julie stepped out of the elevator into the now-empty hall.

"Don't mind Gina," Jack said, coming out of the elevator beside her. "It's not every day that someone returns from the dead." He squeezed her hand. Oh, wow, Jack was holding her hand! This cute, ancient, famous boy was holding her hand! She'd never had a boy hold her hand before. Okay, maybe for gym class in elementary school or something, but never in middle school . . . For an instant, all thoughts of pumpkins, glass slippers, and apple coaches were driven out of her mind. "Don't worry," he said. "We'll get it all sorted out. Your mom and grandma will be fine." He smiled at her, a nice warm smile that felt like a hug. He'll fix everything, Julie thought. Everything really will be fine.

Feeling better, she stepped inside his apartment—and saw cows. Cow-print rug, cow-print couch, cow posters, cow plates on the coffee table, cow figurines on the bookshelf. Even the lamp was a ceramic cow. "We were aiming for classy," Jack said. He raised his voice and called to the kitchen, "You can come out." To Julie he said, "Meet my other roommate."

A cow stuck her head out of the kitchen.

Jack lived with a *cow*? Well, that certainly fit the theme—and Jack's fairy tale. He'd sold his cow for five magic beans. She guessed the cow had forgiven him. "Um, hi," Julie said, trying not to stare. "Nice to meet you."

The cow nodded politely and said, "Moooo."

As the cow retreated back into the kitchen, Julie couldn't help grinning. Everything about this apartment (and about Jack himself) felt friendly and warm and safe. Maybe things were going to be okay now. Dad would listen to Jack and Gina. They'd all return to Northboro, de-pumpkinize Mom and Grandma, and cut back the Wild before it grew too strong. It couldn't have grown too much from just one, okay, *two* fairy-tale moments. And so what if a few tourists had photographed her and Dad in Times Square? No one knew their names or where they lived. A couple of photos by random strangers were no big deal. She shrugged out of her coat—and saw her face on TV.

She froze. Oh, no. The coat fell out of her hands to lie limp on the floor.

Across the room, Dad yanked his duffel bag away from Gina. "I am sorry, but I cannot 'make myself comfortable.' There is a damsel in distress!"

"Oh, my, how distressing," Gina said, laughing. Her laugh faded as she saw Dad's expression. "But you're serious!" She patted his shoulder. "I'm sure Rose isn't really in danger. It must be a misunderstanding."

Julie wished she were misunderstanding what she was seeing. On NBC, reporters were interviewing witnesses who had seen the apple coach and the glass slipper and the birds . . . "Were Dad and I *both* on the news?" Julie cried. "Did everyone see us?"

*Buzz.*

"The horn summons us to battle!" Dad cried. Crouching, he reached for his sword.

"It's only a doorbell," Gina said comfortingly. "Wow, you really are new to this world. You'll get used to it. Just give it time."

The doorbell buzzed again.

"Mooo!" the cow called from the kitchen.

Jack opened the apartment door and in walked a second prince.

He was very nearly a mirror image of Dad, except his cheeks were smooth and flawless—no thorn scars. He'd dyed his hair oil-slick black, and he wore a too-tight T-shirt and tight black jeans with strategically placed, factory-made rips. He looked as if he'd spent hours trying to look as if he'd only spent five minutes getting dressed. Behind him waddled a short and plump woman in a shimmery chiffon blouse and a flare skirt. The plump woman shrieked at Dad, "Ooh, it's you! I saw you on TV!" Julie winced. Guess they *were* both on the news.

Dad bowed. "And it is you, the fairy who, once upon a

time, saved Sleeping Beauty by transforming the curse of death into a spell of sleep."

She waved her hand. "Oh, old news. But you! Out of the Wild after all this time! However did you keep your sanity through the years?" She clapped her hands over her mouth. "Oh my goodness, how rude of me! I shouldn't have assumed you are sane."

*Rude* was definitely the right word. She hadn't so much as glanced at Julie. "He's fine," Julie snapped. Or maybe he wasn't. He had left his true love behind as a pumpkin. "We just need to go home." Once they were home, everything would be okay. The pumpkin spell would end at midnight, and Dad and Mom would be reunited. They'd chop back the Wild, and that would be it.

Sleeping Beauty's fairy spun around at Julie's voice. "Ooh, you must be Julie! Look at you!" Rushing forward, she pinched Julie's cheeks. Julie winced as the fairy squeezed and wiggled her face. Why did all fairies have to be so . . . perky? "Last time I saw you, you were a baby. I came to bestow a gift, but your mom said no." She pouted, but then she flapped her hands excitedly. "Ooh, I could give you a gift now! I've only enchanted inanimate objects for the last century—you know, talking mirrors, bottomless purses, flying carpets . . . but don't be alarmed, I'm sure I haven't lost my touch. What would you like? Grace? Poise? Voice like an angel?"

Could she turn back time? Erase memories? Or at least delete camera footage? Julie wasn't sure what was going to upset Mom more: the fact that they'd left her as a pumpkin, that they'd fueled the Wild, or that they'd appeared on TV.

"We would like," Dad said, "your assistance in the matter of Sleeping Beauty. We are about to embark on her rescue."

The fairy deflated. "Oh."

From the kitchen, the cow protested: "MOOO!"

Gina smiled brightly. "Actually, we were about to have lunch."

Julie couldn't imagine eating now. Her insides felt like they were churning. "We can't," she said. "We have to get home and make sure that the Wild hasn't grown too much."

Dad bowed to the other prince. "I will, of course, cede leadership to you. Sleeping Beauty is your princess. You must be the one to wake her."

Sleeping Beauty's prince shoved his hands in his jeans pockets. "Uh, I can't. You have to understand: outside the Wild, we don't need our story to change before we can change. Rose and I . . . we knew after the first century that we were turning into two different people. Now Rose has her big lawyer career. And me . . . well, there's someone else."

Rosy cheeks glowing even rosier, the fairy beamed at Sleeping Beauty's prince. One guess who the "someone else" is, Julie thought. She couldn't help smiling. They looked so cute and happy, like an ordinary couple . . . *Ordinary*. Julie gawked, her smile fading as she realized: unlike Bobbi, this fairy didn't have wings. She used to have wings. Somehow, she must have removed them.

"Unfathomable," Dad said.

Wow, to give up wings . . .

Jack slung his arm up around Gina's shoulders. "We've found our own happily-ever-afters," he said. They were a couple too, Julie suddenly realized. Gina must have noticed how nice his laugh was. It *was* very nice, but Julie couldn't help wondering, did Gina ever miss her giant height? Did the fairy ever miss her wings? They'd given up a lot for their happily-ever-afters.

Dad shook his head as if he didn't believe what he was seeing. "This is your reason for forsaking Sleeping Beauty?"

And what was Dad's reason for forsaking his Rapunzel? Only hours after Dad had returned to his true love, he'd run off after a different princess! Julie paused. She didn't like thinking that about Dad. Maybe he thought he was doing the right thing. Or maybe he just hadn't thought before he acted, like when he'd picked up the glass slipper. Her eyes slid back to the TV. It had switched from Times

Square, thank goodness. The screen now read, Breaking News: Trenton, New Jersey.

"Look, I'm sorry," the other prince said. "But I can't get involved. That story was a nightmare for me too. Do you have any idea what it's like to kiss someone who's been asleep for a hundred years? Do you know how much dust can accumulate on someone in that length of time? Not to mention spiderwebs."

"Sleeping Beauty is in peril," Dad said, "and you refuse because you are squeamish?" Squeamish for a reason, Julie thought. Kissing spiderwebs was seriously disgusting.

"Rose is not in danger," Gina said. "Bobbi has no reason to kidnap her. They were always cordial. If we simply ask Bobbi what she's planning—"

Dad interrupted. "We can ask her nothing if we cannot find her. We do not even know in what direction she went."

Julie saw the TV zoom in on a tangle of familiar brown brambles. Thorns, the reporters said, had mysteriously sprouted at a gas station in New Jersey. "South," Julie exclaimed. "She went south!" She pointed to the TV.

"A magic portal," Dad breathed. "Marvelous!"

"See, that's proof that it's not a real kidnapping," Jack said, nodding at the TV screen. "No one would kidnap someone so easy to find." Good point, Julie thought. "I'm still thinking the whole thing—the pumpkin spell, the apple coach, the kidnapping—is a practical joke," Jack insisted.

"Ooh, very possible," the fairy said. "Bobbi thinks she's a whole lot funnier than she is." Her prince nodded in agreement.

"Clearly, there has to be some misunderstanding, and we'll find out what it is," Gina said soothingly. She patted Dad's shoulder again. "As you can see, though, there's no need for you to chase after Sleeping Beauty. We can find her whenever we want simply by looking for thorns. You can go home, spend some time with Zel, and get used to our world."

Dad glared at them. "Your 'world' has muddied your thinking. It is quite simple: she is in danger now, so she must be rescued at once."

"He's still a hero," the other prince said a little wistfully.

The fairy hugged his waist. "So are you, sweet pea."

Sleeping Beauty's prince was right. Dad was still a hero. And he didn't know how to stop being a hero and start being a father and husband. He should never have chased Sleeping Beauty, and he should never have picked up that glass slipper. Yes, someone did have to ask Bobbi for an explanation, but that someone shouldn't be Dad. The other fairy-tale characters could track her down easily enough. He needed to get back to his family and learn how to avoid landing on the evening news.

At least Julie could count on Jack and his friends to talk Dad out of his crazy quest. After giving up so much to lead ordinary lives out of the Wild, they wouldn't want Dad to expose them.

"So be it," Dad said. "I know where to search now. I will complete my quest alone." Swinging his duffel bag over his shoulder, he strode toward the balcony's sliding door—and bumped directly into the glass.

"Wait!" Julie said.

"Open sesame!" he commanded the door. It didn't move. He reached forward and slid it open. Wind rushed inside, as well as the street sounds of cars and voices from eleven stories down.

"No, no, no!" Julie chased after him as he stepped onto the balcony. At that moment, the cow emerged from the kitchen right in Julie's path. Julie smacked into her broad neck.

Julie pushed past the cow and raced out onto the balcony as Dad climbed up the railing, mounted the broomstick, and leapt off the balcony. "Dad!" she screamed. She ran to the railing. "Come back! Don't leave me! Dad!"

He receded into the sky.

## Chapter Six
## *The Fairy's Gift*

Julie flung herself back inside the apartment. They had to catch him! If they were quick enough, they could still avert disaster. "Can any of you fly?" she demanded.

Jack, the giantess, the prince, the wingless fairy, and the cow all stared at her.

"Moo," the cow said.

"Anyone *have* anything that can fly? Broomstick? Magic carpet? Hot air balloon? Dragon, griffin . . . anyone, anything?" Why weren't they moving? Each second, Dad was flying farther and farther away. What if he hit a plane? What if he crashed into a building? What if he got lost and . . .

"He hasn't changed a bit," Sleeping Beauty's prince said, his voice full of admiration. "Rapunzel used to be able to rein him in, but no one else could." Julie caught her breath. Of course he hadn't changed! He'd been in the Wild for the last five hundred years. How could he have changed?

"Ten bucks says he shows up here with Sleeping Beauty tomorrow morning," Jack said. The cow mooed in agreement.

Grabbing her coat, Julie glared at them. How could her dad leave her here with these people? How could he leave her behind at all? Was he so unused to having a daughter that he'd forgotten about her entirely? "We can't wait until tomorrow morning! Don't you get it? He doesn't know anything about modern life. He doesn't know how to blend in!"

"He'll manage," Gina said. "*I* managed." Her voice was stiff. Jack squeezed her hand, and the former giantess shivered as if shaking off a bad memory.

Yes, yes, Julie was sure it had been very traumatic, but that wasn't the problem now. She wanted to scream at them. Why didn't they get it? "You left the Wild five hundred years before TVs or phones or the Internet. So a peasant saw you, so what? What if someone spots Dad, calls CNN, and he ends up flying a broomstick on the evening news? What if someone interviews him when he lands?" Julie was shaking as she shouted. She'd never talked to grown-ups this way before. Jaws slack, they stared at her, but she plunged on. She had to make them understand. "He doesn't know how to keep our secret. He doesn't understand *why* we're secret. And even if he did, he doesn't know enough to avoid police or reporters. It won't matter if you don't have wings or aren't a hundred feet tall once Dad starts talking. You won't be safe in your classy cow-themed apartment anymore."

For an instant, there was silence. Julie felt her face flush tomato red. Had she gone too far?

"I'm sorry, Gina," Jack said, releasing her hand, "but the kid is right." Yes! *Kid?* "We can't let him wander around by himself out there."

"Moo," the cow agreed.

Julie exhaled and felt her knees wobble. Good. Very, very good. They were going to go after Dad. She sagged against the wall as the grown-ups began to discuss logistics. "I can enchant the carpet to fly," the fairy said. She pointed at the cow-patterned rug.

Gina shook her head. "We'd be seen," she said. "We should drive. He's chasing the coach, so he'll be following roads anyway."

"So, who has wheels?" Jack asked.

As they argued about transportation, Gina patted Julie on the shoulder. "We'll have everything sorted out soon," she said. "Why don't you grab a bite to eat before we hit the road? Or use the bathroom?" Julie began to protest, but Gina cut her off. "Don't worry, sweetie. We'll find him. All we need to do is follow the thorns, remember?"

Fine. But if they didn't leave in two minutes, she'd . . . She wasn't sure what she was going to do. Something. Julie ducked into the closet-sized bathroom. The shower curtain had a picture of a pasture, of course, and the toilet sported a black-and-white cow-pattern seat. She listened to the fairy-tale characters argue and tried not to worry. Every minute it took to bring Dad back was another minute until someone checked on the Wild. Was it still small enough to cut back? Had it eaten her entire house? Was Boots okay? Was Gillian?

Julie heard the doorbell buzz. Not more people! How many friends had Gina invited? She'd better make sure the new additions didn't slow them down. Pulling her coat on, she put her hand on the doorknob as a muffled voice said, "Police."

She froze.

Oh, no.

She heard footsteps, a door creak, and a cut-off "moo"— they were hiding the cow. "Stay there," she heard Jack say in a quiet voice. He was right outside the bathroom door. Julie backed away from the door and bumped up against the toilet.

"Gentlemen!" Gina said brightly. "How can we help you?"

"We had a report of an . . . incident on your balcony."

Julie didn't breathe. An incident on the balcony. Dad. They'd seen Dad.

"No incident here, sorry," Gina said. "Balcony is totally

fine. Maybe you want the apartment upstairs?" Julie heard a thump. Maybe Gina had tried to shut the door, and the policeman had stopped it? Or maybe the cow had fallen over.

"Our informant specifically cited this apartment." Informant? What informant? Julie thought of the cabdriver, the hundreds of people in Times Square, the pedestrians on the sidewalk below . . . It could have been anyone. The number of people who had seen Dad act like a fairy-tale character was frightening. "A man was seen jumping from your apartment balcony."

"Oh my goodness," Gina cried, her voice ringing with sincerity. "Someone jumped from a balcony? Was he hurt? It's eleven stories! How could anyone—"

"Please don't play games with me, ma'am," the policeman interrupted. "This man flew from your balcony on a broomstick."

Julie heard laughter. It sounded real. She wondered how many times they'd faced situations like this before. How often did they have to pretend that something extraordinary hadn't just happened? "A broomstick?" Jack sputtered. "Wait—I know. The guys at the office sent you. You're not really cops."

Though her heart was thudding against her rib cage, Julie smiled. Wow, they were good. Maybe they would make it through this. Maybe the policemen would leave without investigating any further.

"We have a warrant to search your apartment," a second voice said.

Oh, no. Out in the apartment, the laughter died. Julie backed up against the shower curtain. She had to hide. Where? Behind the shower curtain? In the tub?

"Search for what?" she heard Jack say. "You think we have *magic beans in the medicine cabinet* or something?"

Magic beans. Medicine cabinet. Jack was giving her a message—she couldn't let anyone find the beans! Julie sprang out of the shower and opened the medicine cabinet. Tylenol. Deodorant. NyQuil. She rooted through the shelf. Beans, beans . . .

"Sir! There's a *cow* in the closet!"

She heard a shrill "Moo!"

"Don't hurt her!" Jack cried.

Scuffled footsteps. "I'm placing all of you under arrest—"

"So we violated our lease," Gina said. "We're allowed to have a pet. She's just a little over the poundage limit. You can't arrest us for that!"

Hands shaking, Julie kept searching through the cabinet. If the police found an actual fairy-tale item here, Jack and Gina would never be able to talk their way out of this . . . Julie spotted a small unmarked medicine bottle filled with lima-bean-sized beans. Yes! As she pulled it out, she knocked other pill bottles off the shelf. They fell and clattered in the sink. She froze.

"Who's in the bathroom?"

Her heart thumped wildly. Oh, no, no, no. Footsteps, and then the doorknob rattled. "Open up!" the voice said. "We know you're in there!"

What should she do? What could she do? She shoved the pill bottle into her coat pocket. "Just a minute!" she said. Think, Julie, think! She lunged for the toilet and flushed. You couldn't get arrested for having to pee, right?

"She's just a kid," Jack said. "You don't need to arrest her."

"Come out, kid," the man said.

Trying to make her voice sound even younger, she said, "Am I in trouble?" She didn't have to fake her voice shaking. It shook on its own.

"You're scaring her," the fairy said. "She didn't do anything wrong. It's not like she's in there riding around on a *flying carpet*."

"Hey, what was that?" one man said.

"What?" the other said.

"I saw sparkles . . ."

Julie felt a tug under her feet. She looked down. Sparkles swarmed over her sneakers. The bath mat writhed underneath her. Suddenly, it shot up. Julie fell off it backward as it spurted out from under her.

The fairy had enchanted the bath mat!

Quickly, Julie threw open the bathroom window, stepped onto the toilet seat, and grabbed the flying bath mat. She swung herself on. Behind her, the lock popped out on the bathroom door. Flattening onto her stomach, Julie zoomed out the window as the bathroom door burst open.

## Chapter Seven
### Zel

Zel heard buzzing. She opened her eyes to find her face pressed against an orange shag rug. What was she doing—

Bobbi's wand! She'd been enchanted!

She tried to leap to her feet. Several hands grabbed her arm. "Steady! Steady! You've been a pumpkin. Take it slow." Zel focused in on the speaker: one of Snow White's seven dwarves. He helped her stand.

Zel frowned at him. "You were asleep," she said groggily. She looked around. All seven dwarves were now awake, and the thorn brambles had withered to a mat of scattered leaves. She shook her head, feeling as if she was clearing away a fog. Why were the dwarves awake? Why had the thorns died? "Did someone wake Sleeping Beauty?"

"She was either awakened or moved," Gothel said behind her. "The thorns would fade in either case."

Where was Prince? And where was Julie? Zel looked

around, and her heart squeezed. She didn't see Julie. Where was she? "Julie? Julie!" Zel took a step toward the door. Her head spun, and the buzzing sound switched to frantic beeping.

One of Snow's seven slapped an alarm clock, and the beeping stopped. "We tricked the spell," he explained. "We changed the clock to midnight and set the alarm—when the clock 'struck' twelve, you woke."

"Clever," Gothel said admiringly.

Walk, Zel commanded her legs. Walk! She hobbled to the door. "Julie!" She turned back to Snow's seven. "Where did she go? Is she okay?"

The dwarves hesitated and looked at each other. "There were only two pumpkins when we woke," one of them said.

Zel felt cold. Only two . . . She clutched the side of the door. "Julie!" She turned back to her mother and the dwarves. "Maybe she was turned into something else. Help me look," she commanded.

Gothel yanked sheets off the bed and overturned pillows. "When I find that fairy godmother," she said, "I am turning her into a cockroach."

"If she so much as touched one hair on Julie's head, I'll help you," Zel said, fighting to keep the fear out of her voice. Julie had to be okay. She had to be. Maybe they had gone for help. Maybe she and Prince had gone home. Hurrying to the motel room phone, Zel wiped her sweating palms on her pants and dialed the house.

One ring. Two. Three. Four . . . The answering machine should be picking up. Why wasn't it picking up? Julie, Julie, Julie, please be all right! Why wasn't Boots answering? Prince had cut through the thorns to reach Sleeping Beauty. Was that enough of a fairy-tale moment to cause the Wild to grow? Had the Wild covered enough of the house to cut off the phone?

"I'll turn her into a cockroach and drop her into the sewer," Gothel promised.

Oh, God, what if Julie had gone home and the Wild had grown while she was there? Legs still shaking, Zel ran for her car. "Search here!" she called over her shoulder.

"Take my broomstick!" Gothel called. "I'll get it!"

"It's daylight!" Zel objected. "People will see!" But Gothel didn't listen to her. She darted into the motel lobby to fetch her broom as Zel unlocked her car.

As Zel shoved the key into the ignition, Gothel burst back outside. "My broomstick is gone! That fairy godmother"—she said the name like an insult—"stole it!"

Bobbi wouldn't have stolen her broomstick. What did a fairy godmother need with a witch's broomstick? She had wings. Plus she could instantly zap herself from place to place. She didn't need any kind of help in the transportation department.

Julie could have taken it, Zel thought. She could have used it to go for help! Maybe she'd taken her father with her.

"Wait," Gothel said. "I'll find my spare."

"I'm going," Zel said. "Don't fly. You'll make things worse. If Julie's okay, the last thing she needs is for us to draw attention to her." She slammed the car door shut and then zoomed out of the Wishing Well Motel parking lot with a screech. She gripped the steering wheel so hard that her knuckles hurt. Please, please, please, let her be okay, she thought.

How far had the Wild grown? How many people had it swallowed? How fast was it spreading? How had everything gone so very wrong? Her prince had returned, and Zel had lost him in less than an hour. How had that happened?

It should have been perfect. He was free! Miracle of miracles, the Wild had set him free! She shouldn't have cared how or why. She should have been like Julie and basked in the absolute wonder of the miracle. But Zel couldn't. She had to be the sensible one, always the planner, always the general. She had to worry about how the world would react. She had to fight with him before he'd been out of the Wild even a day.

Zel eased up on the gas pedal. Now was not the time to be stopped for speeding. Even now, she had to be cautious. Don't draw attention. Blend in with the crowd.

She should have known that Prince would have refused to blend in. He wasn't made to blend. He was made to shine. It was one of the things she had loved about him from the beginning. He had come to her tower like a ray of sunshine. Zel swallowed a lump in her throat. For a moment, she'd had that sunshine again. She could still feel his arms around her, and she could still see the way his eyes blazed warm and bright when he looked at her. Where was he now? What had Bobbi done with him? And why?

Up ahead, near the turn onto Crawford Street, Zel saw brake lights. She slowed to a halt. Rising in her seat, she saw the flash of red and blue police lights reflecting off SUVs and cars at the turnoff. Please let it be construction. She waited for a minute, tapping her fingers on the steering wheel.

The cars didn't budge.

They weren't going anywhere, she realized. Zel undid her seat belt, opened the car door, and stepped out. She couldn't see anything from here. Stepping on the driver's seat, Zel climbed onto the car roof. Squatting, she balanced on the curved roof of her Volkswagen. Horns honked. Someone yelled at her to get back in her car. She ignored them. You have to look, she told herself. You have to know. Slowly, Zel stood.

Wind whipped through her hair. She felt the chill of the December air and tasted car exhaust on her tongue.

Looking over the cars and across roofs of houses and the twisted leafless trees, she saw dark lush summer green rising up in the direction of home. Her hands clenched into fists. She wanted to scream. She wanted to choke every leaf, uproot every tree, and burn every branch. Another gust of wind slapped her, but she planted her feet firmly on the car roof.

The Wild couldn't have this world. She wouldn't let it. Not this time.

"Zel, is that you?" a voice said. "Are you all right?"

Fists still clenched, she looked down. Leaning on Zel's open car door, Linda the librarian waved at her, her normally cheery face now filled with concern. Behind her, several other drivers had stepped out of their cars. All of them wanted to see what Zel was looking at. Some were on their cell phones. She saw a kid climb onto the roof of an SUV and point toward the Wild.

"It's back," Zel said to Linda. "But you're happy about that, aren't you?" She heard how her voice sounded but couldn't stop it: angry, dark, ugly. Linda had caused the Wild to escape with her irresponsible wish. She had nearly destroyed Zel's world, including her daughter. Julie, where are you? she thought. Are you up ahead? Are you back in the Wild?

"I don't know what you mean," Linda said, doe-eyed. Underneath her coat, she was wearing, Zel noticed, a pink shirt with silver glitter that said, Northboro: Fairy-Tale Capital of the World. Zel heard a roaring in her ears. She hated, hated, *hated* those tourist shirts, that casual attitude, that lack of understanding . . .

Zel thrust her hand down. "Come up and see for yourself."

"On the roof?" Linda wrinkled her nose, but when Zel didn't reply, she took Zel's hand and climbed up on top of the car. Zel helped her steady her balance, and then she pointed wordlessly toward the writhing green that now towered over Crawford Street. "Ooh, wow," Linda said. "How exciting!"

Exciting? "You're an idiot," Zel said flatly. It felt good to say it. She kept going. "You're an irresponsible, witless ninny who messed with forces beyond your comprehension. You caused this last time. You gave it its taste of freedom. And now it's back, and you don't even have the intelligence to recognize this for the catastrophe it is." Grabbing Linda's arm, Zel pointed again at the Wild, trying to force her to see it for the nightmare it was. Silhouetted against the clear blue sky, the green stretched and swayed as if it wanted to claw out the sun. "*That* is the Wild. It will swallow the world if it can. It will destroy every life it touches." Linda yelped, and Zel released her. She took a deep breath. This time, it isn't Linda's fault, she thought. It's mine. I let everything spiral out of control. I let Prince keep his sword, and he used it to chop through the thorns. I let Bobbi surprise me with a spell, and the Wild was able to grow unchecked. "I know you didn't do it this time."

"I wasn't even in the motel when your prince cut through the thorns," Linda said, massaging her arm. "Or in New York when he fit the glass slipper on the Cinderella wannabe."

"I know," Zel said. "I'm sorry. I . . ." She stopped. Glass slipper? What glass slipper? What was Prince doing in New York? And how did Linda know about the thorns? Only Zel, Julie, Prince, Gothel, and Bobbi had been there.

Linda smiled at her.

Zel felt a tightening in the pit of her stomach.

"It's a good spell, isn't it?" Linda said. "I don't even recognize myself."

A good spell . . . Zel shook her head, not believing what she was hearing.

"Your mother isn't the only witch, you know," Linda continued. "Snow's stepmother also knows a few tricks. Remember how she transformed herself into an old peddler woman to trick Snow into eating the poisoned apple? Her spell only required a few modifications to disguise me."

Zel felt her heart hammer in her chest. Linda wasn't . . . She couldn't be a fairy-tale character! Zel knew all the fairy-tale characters. She would have known . . .

"You don't even know me now, do you?" Linda said.

But . . . but Linda had made the wish in the well that brought the Wild back. No one who had been in the Wild would ever do that. She couldn't be one of them! "Who are you?" Zel's voice was a whisper.

"Five hundred years ago, we fought for you," Linda said. "You were our general, and we all worshipped you. You were so sure of yourself, so sure you knew what was best for everyone."

"I don't understand," Zel said. Who was Linda? Why had she made a wish in the well? What did she want now? Did this have anything to do with Bobbi's betrayal at the motel? "Bobbi . . ."

"Bobbi works for me now," Linda said. "And she's not the only one."

Zel was stunned. Bobbi worked for Linda? Doing what? Transforming her friends into pumpkins? *Why?* "My daughter," Zel said. "Where's Julie?" If anything had . . .

"I am sorry for this," Linda said softly, even kindly, "but since you didn't stay a pumpkin and since I can't have you interfering . . ." She looked over Zel's shoulder and gave a nod.

It might have been five hundred years since her last battle, but Zel knew a signal when she saw one. She spun and crouched in a single motion, keeping her balance on the car roof. She saw nothing. Tricked!

Before she could react, Linda's hand shot in front of her face, and Zel saw a flash of red as something slammed against her mouth. She tasted cool, wet sweetness as the juice from Snow White's poisoned apple dripped into her throat.

## Chapter Eight
### *The Flying Bath Mat*

Shooting out of the apartment window, the flying bath mat careened down, down, down toward the New York street below. Shrieking, Julie yanked back hard on the front fringe. The bath mat zoomed up, up, up over roofs and water towers, past windows and fire escapes and scaffolding. Cold wind whistled in her ears. Julie flattened spread-eagle, and the bath mat leveled out.

Oh, wow. That was . . . wow. Close. Scary. Cool.

Below her, Manhattan sprawled in all directions. She saw Central Park, a swathe of winter brown and evergreen amid skyscrapers, and for an instant, she forgot about Dad, about Jack, about Sleeping Beauty, about Mom and Grandma, about the Wild. She was flying over New York City! Somehow, this felt different from clinging to Dad while he flew the broomstick. This time, it was just her with the wind in her face and sun on her back, flying like the birds . . . flying *with* the birds. Up ahead, she saw a flock of pigeons—and a man on a broomstick.

Dad! But shouldn't he be miles and miles from here by now? On the other hand, who else would be riding a broomstick over Manhattan? "Come on, go faster," she ordered the bath mat. It darted forward. "Dad!" she shouted.

"Julie!" he said, reining in his broomstick. "Why have you followed me?"

What? No "sorry I abandoned you"? No "happy you escaped"? No "I was just going to rescue you"? "Jack and Gina and everyone—they're all being arrested right now," she said. "We have to go back and help them!"

"I am already on a quest," he said with real regret in his voice, "and Sleeping Beauty needs me more. Your mother would never respect a prince who left a damsel in distress."

"No more questing!" Julie said. "Don't you see that there are people who need you *here*? Please, Dad, we need to go back." How could she make him understand? Jack, Gina, the cow—they'd built lives here. The fairy had even sacrificed her wings so she could lead a normal life. Dad had destroyed all that without a single thought. He had to help them. "We have to help Jack and Gina and the others, and then we have to go home and help Mom."

"I cannot return to Rapunzel without Sleeping Beauty," he said. "But I have found help. Cinderella's birds will lead us to her." He gestured to the flock of pigeons.

Did he know there was such a thing as ordinary birds? All his life, he'd been surrounded by magic. The amount he didn't know about the real world was staggering—and dangerous. "Not all birds here are magical," Julie called. The wind began to pick up. Gripping the fringes of the bath mat, she rode the gusts. "The birds in Times Square were totally an exception!" She had to shout over the roar of the wind.

"Your skies are full of magical birds!" Dad shouted back, and pointed behind Julie. "See, a hollow bird with living men inside it!"

She turned the bath mat. In front of her, a helicopter rose up between the skyscrapers. Wind pummeled her face. She squinted and saw the words *Channel 7, Eye from the Sky*, emblazoned on the side and the wide lens of a TV camera pointed directly at her.

Julie felt her stomach drop as if she'd plummeted a thousand feet. Oh, no, no, no. She and Dad were being filmed flying! They could be on the news right now. Thousands could be watching. Millions! "Go!" Julie shouted. She raced ahead, and Dad swung his broomstick around to follow.

Julie rocketed past the pigeons. In minutes, the thrum of the helicopter blades fell behind her. She looked back over her shoulder to see it receding with the New York skyline. She wanted to cheer. A helicopter couldn't match the speed of a magical broomstick and bath mat.

Soon, they were alone in the sky, sailing over lower

Manhattan, over a wide river, and then over a sea of power plants and oil tanks. Only when the highway split into six lanes and Julie saw signs to Trenton did she realize that they had flown south into New Jersey. Looking back again, she didn't see a trace of the helicopter, which was good, but she should have fled north. South was not—

"The birds were correct!" Dad said. Aiming down, he plummeted.

"Dad, what are you doing?" she shrieked. Was he crazy? He was going to get hit! There were cars and trucks and buses and . . . He whipped between them, skimming low over the asphalt. "Watch out!" Leaning forward, she swooped down. She heard the whoosh, whoosh, whoosh of cars as she zipped past them.

Just ahead of her, Dad flew over a wide crack in the road. Brown brambles filled the crack. They punched through the asphalt, spilling over the black pavement like a thousand worms.

Sleeping Beauty's thorns. He'd actually found them. She couldn't believe it. Had Dad been right? Had those pigeons been helpful fairy-tale birds? Or was this just a coincidence? A truck honked behind her, and she swerved. "Okay, fine, you found the thorns! Please, go up!" Julie begged.

"We have the trail now!" he said. "Onward!" As if he rode a horse instead of a broomstick, he reared back, and then he soared up into the sky.

"Dad, wait for me!" Julie chased after him.

Following the New Jersey Turnpike, they swooped around cell phone towers and over green exit signs. Below, the city of Philadelphia flashed by, and then the green signs counted down to Baltimore, and then to Washington, DC.

Urging her bath mat higher, Julie saw the Washington Monument and the dome of the Capitol Building in the distance, silhouetted against blue sky. This, she thought, is like some bizarre dream. She shouldn't be flying past DC on a bath mat. She shouldn't be on a quest at all. This was the real world, not the Wild. Here, magic was hidden. Spells were secret. But Dad was turning that all upside down.

They flew over rolling hills so high that mist was trapped between them, and then they turned west over farms, towns, and sprawling cities. They stopped as needed to use bathrooms at gas stations, and Julie bought pretzels and other snacks from vending machines with coins she had in her pockets. At each stop, she tried to convince Dad to turn around and go home. At each stop, he refused. And they flew on.

\* \* \*

As the sun set over western Tennessee, Dad suddenly cried, "Victory!" Jerking the front of his broomstick, he braked in mid-air.

Zooming past him, Julie squeezed the front fringe of her bath mat and shouted, "Whoa, whoa, whoa!" Amazingly, it worked. She guided the bath mat back to where Dad circled high above a sprawling house . . . or at least what used to be a house. Now it was a tangle of brown brambles and thorns.

"We have found her!" Dad announced.

So had a string of police cars, a few news vans, and several hundred people.

Dad angled his broom toward the house. He could *not* be serious. Julie darted in front of him. "Dad, we can't let all those people see us flying!" Not that a zillion drivers hadn't seen them already . . . Still, she had to try.

To her surprise, Dad agreed readily. "Of course. We do not want them to think us witches." Veering away, he glided down to a landing on a side street. Julie skidded to a halt on a manicured lawn beside him.

Dad stuffed his broomstick and her bath mat into the duffel bag next to the sword and then zipped the bag, leaving the hilt of his sword exposed—so he could draw it quickly? "Please tell me you aren't planning to use your sword," Julie said, but he was already marching down the street. She hurried to keep up.

One block and one turn later, she saw the house.

"We found her!" Dad said, beaming.

Sleeping Beauty was very clearly inside. Roses wound

up the front pillars. Thick **knots** of thorns obscured the roof. Brambles covered **the window**s. Following Dad, Julie wormed through the crowd to get a better view of the house, encased in a fairy-tale barrier.

People posed their kids in front of the main gate, which was curved to look like sheet music with giant musical notes plastered across it. But the people weren't taking photos of the fancy gate; they were taking photos of Sleeping Beauty's thorns, framed by the rosy sunset. Julie heard excited whispers: "Just like Massachusetts!" Camera flashes winked all around her.

She could have told them it wasn't the same. This wasn't the Wild. It wouldn't expand beyond the house. It wouldn't try to take over the world. If Sleeping Beauty woke or was moved, it would wither and die. But to the crowd, it must have looked the same. So why weren't they running for their lives? Why did they all seem so . . . so happy?

And why were there so many people here anyway? What *was* this place?

Scanning the crowd around her, Julie saw a boy about her age looking at her. He had green eyes. Really nice green eyes. He squeezed behind a man with a camera to stand next to Julie. She felt herself blush. She hated when she blushed. She felt like a plump, red tomato. For an instant, faced with the Cutest Boy Ever, Julie forgot about Dad, Sleeping Beauty, and the fairy godmother.

"Tours were canceled," he said.

"Huh?" she said, and then blushed again. Couldn't she think of anything more intelligent to say? Maybe "tours of what"?

"You were here for the tour, right? We came for the tour. Dad and me. I always wanted to see this place. Dad used to play his stuff when I was real little. I know, kinda weird lullaby, but that's Dad."

Julie stared at him. Wow, he talked fast. "Um, what is this place?" she asked.

The boy blinked at her. For a second, he didn't speak. Julie wondered what she'd said wrong, but then he said, "Graceland. Elvis's home. You know, the King."

Now it was her turn to blink at him. "You're kidding." Sleeping Beauty was inside *Graceland*? How weird was that? Sleeping Beauty and Elvis? It sounded like a tabloid headline. Why on earth had Bobbi brought her here of all the million, billion possible places?

"Did you say this is a king's home?" Dad asked.

Julie jumped. She hadn't realized he'd been listening.

"Yeah, he really lived here," the boy gushed. "Cool, huh? And it's supposedly exactly the way it was when he lived here. Not just the museum part. Even the upstairs, which is totally off-limits to the public so there's no museum reason to keep it the same, except that it's cool that nothing's been touched since he died. He supposedly died right there on the bathroom floor." He pointed up at the second floor but kept right on talking as if he was worried he'd run out of oxygen before he could finish. "And they just preserved everything. Well, not *him*. They buried him, of course. That would be just gross. But I heard it's all exactly the same, as if he were going to one day just wake up and start living here again."

Julie shivered. Put that way, it seemed perfectly appropriate that Sleeping Beauty was here. This mansion was frozen in time just like her castle had been in the original story. But why did Bobbi need to kidnap her to bring her here? Why not just ask Mom? Why turn Mom and Grandma into pumpkins? It didn't make sense.

"You know, you're, like, the only person within thirty years of my age that I've seen since we got here," the boy said.

Julie was still thinking about Bobbi. If this had been her destination all along, why hadn't she simply poofed herself here? Why transform an apple and mice and cross hundreds of miles . . .

"You here with your dad?" he asked.

Staring at Graceland, Julie almost didn't hear the question. "Y-yes," she said.

He nodded. "Me too. Total surprise trip. How cool is that? Dad just said pack, and we jumped in the RV and here we are. He has a whole itinerary planned: here, Grand Canyon, Disneyland. Early birthday present."

"Happy birthday," she said absently.

"We must speak with this king," Dad said. "It is always wise to enlist the aid of local royalty. Once I wake Sleeping Beauty, it will be good to have assistance when I face her kidnapper."

Julie felt her face turn bright red as the cutest boy who had ever talked to her stared at her father like he was crazy. "Are you guys from Massachusetts?" he asked. "I heard everyone there thought they were in a fairy tale. Weird stuff."

"Yeah," she said. "Weird."

A voice behind the boy said, "Henry, who are you talking to?"

Henry. The Cutest Boy Ever was named Henry. Henry turned, and Julie saw a very short man, so short that he could have been a cousin of Snow's seven. The man—Henry's father, Julie guessed—was about as tall as Henry's armpit. But that was where the resemblance to Snow's seven ended. He was beardless and wore an Elvis shirt. Snow's seven would never have worn an Elvis shirt. They didn't approve of any music more recent than Mozart (whom they had known personally). "Hi, I'm Julie," she said.

"Rumpelstiltskin!" Dad said.

Julie froze. He didn't just say that. Please, let him not have just said that.

Drawing himself up, the man planted his fists on his

hips. "Do I walk up to you and insult your height or hair or—"

"Do you not know me, Rumpelstiltskin?" Dad said. "I am Rapunzel's prince."

Julie jumped in. "I'm so sorry," she said. "Please excuse my dad. He's had a rough time lately." You could define "lately" as the last five hundred years, right?

Dad frowned in confusion. "I meant no offense. Rumpelstiltskin was a great friend of mine. Much misunderstood by my royal cousins. You do look very much like him."

Okay, not helping.

The man scowled. "Let's go, Henry."

And then the Cutest Boy Ever followed his dad away and was quickly swallowed by the crowd. Julie stood on tiptoes trying to see where he went, but he was gone. She turned back to Dad, about to explain (again) why he shouldn't mention fairy tales . . .

Dad drew his sword. "You stay here, Julie. I must pass this gate."

Whoa, no sword! Bad sword! "Dad, no, put that away!" She grabbed his arm. He couldn't be planning to hack his way through! He was not, not, *not* going to re-create another fairy-tale moment!

At least Henry hadn't stayed to see this. If he thought Dad was crazy before . . . Julie glanced at the crowd to make sure he was gone. He was. Unfortunately, others had seen. All the tourists around them had backed away, leaving Dad in an empty circle of sidewalk. A reporter elbowed his way through the crowd toward Julie and Prince. "Let me through! Press coming through! Press!" He shoved a microphone in Dad's face. "Sir, can you comment on—"

"I must reach the castle," Dad interrupted in a voice that brokered no argument. He eyed the reporter and the cameraman. "The crowd parted for you and your . . . giant eye." He nodded at the camera. "If you will part the throng again, then I shall rescue the princess." Julie shot a quick look at the camera. A red light flashed on the top. Did that mean it was taping? Had Dad's words just been broadcast to the entire world? I have to stop this, she thought. How do I stop this? She wished Mom were here. Mom would know what to do.

"Sure, we can get you closer," the reporter said in a much friendlier voice.

Before Julie could do anything, the reporter and cameraman flanked Dad and shepherded him around the tourists and through the front gate. Julie scurried to keep up.

"I want an exclusive," the reporter said, all chummy now. "You're from Northboro, aren't you? The Fairy-Tale Capital of the World. You've seen this all before."

"Indeed I have," Prince said.

At the reporter's signal, the cameraman scooted around

for a better shot of the prince with the thorn-encrusted Graceland behind him. Dad handed the duffel bag to Julie. "Please await my return."

She swung the bag over her shoulder. "If I can't stop you, then I'm at least coming with you."

A policeman sauntered forward to intercept. "Sir, I have to ask you to go back behind the gate." He had a Southern drawl. He also had a gun. His hand rested lightly on it, and his eyes were trained on Dad's sword.

Oh, no, Dad wouldn't know what a gun was. Would he even recognize a policeman? What if Dad tried to fight?

"I am here to help," Dad said. His voice was like milk chocolate, smooth and certain. It was the voice of someone you shouldn't doubt.

The policeman took his hand off his gun and (to Julie's surprise) smiled.

Wow, Julie thought. First the reporter and now the policeman. She hadn't considered what it meant for a prince to be charming. This was Dad's kind of magic: his voice seemed to say, "Trust me. I am here to save you."

The policeman shook his head. In an apologetic voice, he said, "We've tried to cut through it—"

Stepping up to the house, Prince hacked at a thorny vine, and it melted away from the blade. "Be right back!" Julie called to the policeman. She grabbed the back of Dad's shirt and plunged in with him.

Brambles closed around them. Julie felt bark slither around her ankles, and she tried not to scream. Thorns grazed her skin as the barrier wove itself shut behind her. She clung to Dad's shirt as he swung his sword machete-like through the thorn barrier. Rustling, the vines rearranged themselves, parting for Dad's sword. Light from the setting sun filtered down in fractured streaks, and the sound of the crowd faded behind them.

Suddenly, Dad's sword swished through empty air. In the weak light, Julie saw an opening—the front door to Graceland. Without hesitating, Dad walked through it. Julie glanced back at the thick thorn barrier behind them as she followed Dad inside.

*   *   *

Inside Graceland, it was dark. Shadows, as twisted and tangled as the thorns that blocked the window, coated the King's house. The fading sunlight pierced through in thin, weak slivers. Clutching the back of Dad's shirt, Julie followed him. After the crowd of tourists, the quiet here felt peaceful. It was a sleeping silence.

Julie thumped her shin against something hard. "Ow!" Releasing Dad's shirt, she rubbed her shin and squinted at the shadow in front of her. It was an end table, she guessed. She peered at the room around her. Up ahead, she saw a glint of blue, a stained glass window with images of parrots or maybe peacocks. Beyond the glass, she saw a shiny black shadow. She guessed it was a piano.

Julie saw movement along the walls. "Dad!" she cried. He spun around, and she saw a blur of color as he turned. A mirror, she realized. There were mirrors on the walls. Mirrors everywhere, actually. She'd seen a corner of one, mostly obscured by thorny vines. "Sorry," Julie said. "False alarm."

"I asked you to wait outside," Dad said. "The fairy godmother could be here. How can I keep you safe if you will not obey me?"

Funny. Julie could have said the same thing. If he'd listened to her, he'd have never touched that glass slipper, never have crossed the East Coast, and never have entered a thorn-encrusted Graceland. What were they doing here? They should be home with Mom. They should be back guarding the Wild.

At least they had nearly found Sleeping Beauty. Once they had her, they could load her onto the bath mat, fly home, and then this whole stupid quest would be over. It could become just another story she told Gillian on the phone. Gillian would probably think it was a grand, wonderful adventure. Julie nearly smiled, but then she had a thought. "You know you can't actually kiss her, right?" If his hacking at thorns at the motel had made the Wild grow like she guessed it had, Julie didn't want to think about what kissing the actual Sleeping Beauty would do. "We're just going to take her back to Mom, right? I mean, when we find her. Where *is* she anyway?"

"She'd be in the highest tower," Prince said.

Um, Graceland didn't have a tower. "It's a two-story house," Julie said. The first floor was the museum, and the second floor was off-limits, according to Henry.

"We must find stairs," Dad said. "And hope there are no dragons to guard it."

"Right," Julie said, rolling her eyes. "I always hope that."

Circling through the first floor, they found the staircase by the front entrance—they had passed it initially in the darkness. Narrow rays of light illuminated a velvet rope barrier blocking a curved staircase. On the left side of the staircase, above a row of red potted flowers, hung an over-sized oil painting of Elvis. At the top, a mannequin in a display case sported a black-and-white Elvis suit. Stepping over the rope barrier, Dad charged up the stairs. Julie un-hooked the rope barrier and followed.

Dad halted as the stairs turned. Julie bumped into his back. Peeking around him, she saw a man crumpled on the top step. She clutched the railing as her head spun. Oh, whoa, was he—

He wasn't dead, she realized. He was *snoring*.

Like Snow's seven, this man—a security guard, to judge by his uniform—had been caught inside the thorn barrier and, like in Sleeping Beauty's fairy tale, he had fallen asleep. Julie thought of the sleeping dwarves in Grandma's motel as she and Prince skirted around the guard. Were they still asleep? Had they discovered the two pumpkins? Were Mom and Grandma all right? We have to find Sleeping Beauty and get home *now*, Julie thought.

Upstairs tasted stale. Julie breathed in dust. She was sweating in her coat, especially under the strap of the duffel bag. It was even darker upstairs, thanks to the mansion's black padded walls. They peered first into the room on the left. She saw deep red wallpaper, thick curtains, and the shadows of a desk and chairs—this was an office. No Sleeping Beauty. They checked the room on the right—it was a bedroom, decorated entirely in white and gold.

"She is here," Dad whispered. "I smell roses."

The white and gold bedroom *did* smell of roses. Julie eyed the perfume vials on the vanity and thought that they might have something to do with the scent. She bet that Sleeping Beauty would be in Elvis's room, not here in what was clearly a woman's bedroom. But where was Elvis's room? She hadn't seen an obvious entrance . . . unless that black padded wall at the top of the stairs was actually a door.

As Dad exposed an empty bed, Julie stepped back into the hall. Now that she was looking for it, she could make out the doorknob in the wall. She also saw a chain dangling on one side with an open padlock. That was a promising sign—someone had been here. She tried the doorknob. It turned easily, and she pushed the door open.

Elvis's bedroom was drenched in crimson. Mirrors covered the ceiling. Red draperies scalloped the corners. In the center she saw an enormous bed, larger than king-sized, a sea of scarlet quilt with bulging shadows in the middle. Dropping the duffel bag by the door, she drew closer to the bed.

The shadows looked like . . . Yes, the shadows were in the shape of a person. Sleeping Beauty! She'd found her! "Dad!" she called. "Dad, come here!"

The body in the bed growled.

That didn't sound like Sleeping Beauty.

Julie turned back in time to see a flash of gray fur leap out of the crimson sheets. In the dim light, she saw yellow eyes, sharp teeth, a feral face, the body of a . . . "Wolf!" she yelled. She felt the wolf's breath hot in her face, and she heard herself scream.

The wolf's jaws widened, widened, widened beyond impossibly wide—and clamped down over her head. She felt hot, wet darkness slide around her. Teeth grazed her arms. She screamed again, and the wolf swallowed her whole.

## Chapter Nine
### *The Wolf*

Air! Julie needed air! Thick heat clogged her throat. She clawed around her, and her fingernails raked into sticky softness. The smell of bile and stale blood filled her nose and her mouth. Let me out! Please, let me out! Heat squeezed her lungs. Her ribs pressed into each other. Her knees were jammed up into her chest, and her arms were pinned against her. She scratched and kicked, but the warm, wet walls cocooned her as if she were a fetus in a womb. Let me out! Out, out, out! She couldn't breathe. She felt her head swim. Please, please, please . . .

The walls trembled around her. She heard a horrible scream. No, she *felt* the scream. It shook her from inside out. She couldn't move her arms to cover her ears. The scream penetrated deep into her skull and echoed there. Water gushed—was it water? It felt thick and warm. Thick liquid poured over her, and she saw a shard of light.

The shard of light pierced through the red-black bubbling gush. Julie pushed toward the light as air rushed toward her. She gasped in and then spat as thick salty iron liquid poured into her mouth. She fell onto the floor, coughing and vomiting.

Her dad knelt over her. His sword lay beside him in a pool of . . . oh, God, that was blood. Everywhere, blood. She'd been tasting . . . She retched again, her stomach heaving, and then she felt her dad scoop her into his arms and lift her off the floor. A few seconds later, she heard running water, and she felt a towel on her face. Gently, her dad washed the blood and . . . She didn't want to think what else. She didn't want to think at all. Keeping her eyes closed tight, she let him dab her face with water.

"Are you hurt?" he asked, his voice urgent.

She'd been swallowed alive. Swallowed whole. She'd been inside . . . Julie gritted her teeth. She was not going to be sick again. "I'm okay." Her skin felt like one giant bruise everywhere, and her head buzzed and hummed. But she was alive.

"Good," he said, his voice gentle now. "I will fetch us new clothes. You will feel better once you are clean again."

She opened her eyes. Her lashes felt stuck together as if she were wearing gummy mascara. Blinking, she saw a bathroom, a tacky orange-and-brown tile bathroom with gold fixtures. She was on the floor between the toilet and the shower. Blood-soaked towels lay around her. She tried not to look at them.

Yes, she needed to be clean again. Right now.

Gripping the sink counter, she pulled herself to standing. Her legs unfolded as if they'd been packed together for hours. The sink was still running. Splashing water on her face, she tried not to look in the mirror, but despite her efforts, she caught glimpses of deep red clots in her hair and streaks on her neck. Her clothes were hardening. Her skin shuddered back from the stiffening cotton. She shed her coat. It didn't help. The . . . mess . . . had seeped through her coat to her clothes.

Clean, she thought. Need to be clean.

She stumbled to the shower. Turning the faucets on, she stepped in fully clothed. She stood there and let the steam and water pour over her. She heard Dad enter the room. "I will wait for you outside this door," he said. "Simply speak if you need me." Julie heard the door close as he left. Stripping off her clothes, she scrubbed as if she could clean away what had just happened. Eaten alive. Swallowed whole. Cut out of a wolf's stomach.

Shutting off the shower, she dried herself with a hand towel, the only clean one in the bathroom, and she dressed in a black shirt that hung to her knees and jeans that dragged on the floor. One of Elvis's shirts?

And she had just showered in Elvis Presley's bathroom.

Gillian was never going to believe this, she thought. But the thought failed to make her smile. Instead, she started to shake. She took deep breath after deep breath.

Julie extracted her old belt from her ruined jeans and ran it under the sink faucet until it looked like just a stained brown. She threaded it through the pants and rolled up the jean cuffs. She then emptied out her old pockets and stuffed the contents into her new pants: house key, three nickels and some pennies, old receipts, her school ID, and Gillian's English homework (now more than a little crumpled and stained). She took Jack's bottle of magic beans out of her coat and stuffed it into her oversized jeans pocket. Now fully dressed and clean, she felt almost human again. Stepping over the blood-soaked towels and clothes, she opened the door to the bedroom.

Her father was wearing the black-and-white Elvis suit from the top of the staircase. Rhinestones studded the sleeves, and the pants flared into bell-bottoms. She laughed before she could stop herself, shrill and loud. It shattered the silence of the crimson-draped bedroom, and then her laugh died as she realized that she could now *see* the room. Light from streetlamps shone through the windows.

Dad saw her look at the windows. "The thorns are fading," he said. "Sleeping Beauty has been moved."

"We have to leave," Julie said. "Now." If the thorns were fading, then the police would be coming soon, and the guard on the stairs would wake. They'd find Julie and Prince here in Elvis's bedroom. They'd find blood in Elvis's bedroom and bathroom. They'd find . . . it. Him. She made herself turn and look.

The Wolf—not any wolf, but the original wolf, the ageless fairy-tale wolf—lay still on the thick shag rug of Elvis's bedroom. His jaws were open, and his eyes stared sightlessly at the crimson wall. His stomach had been sliced, and the fur around it was matted with drying blood.

She stared at him and felt dizzy again. "You killed him."

"He ate you," Dad said.

"He isn't coming back," she said. "This isn't the Wild. His tale won't restart. He's *dead*. Gone."

"I would do it again," Dad said, "for you. I will not let anyone harm my daughter, regardless of the consequences." It was the first time since his escape from the Wild that he'd called her "daughter."

She dragged her eyes from the wolf to her father. He no longer looked silly in the old rock-and-roll suit. He looked . . . noble. It was a king's suit, and he wore it like a king. "I could have died," Julie said, hushed.

"I would do it again," he repeated.

She heard noises downstairs. There were people in the house. How long before they discovered the velvet rope that she had unhooked at the base of the stairs? How long before they came to check the second floor?

How long before the guard woke? Was he awake already?

"I don't understand," Julie said. It couldn't have been an accident that the wolf was here inside Sleeping Beauty's thorn barrier. He wasn't lying in bed in the dark by accident. He didn't leap on her and swallow her by accident. This was intentional. This was a trap. The wolf must have come here to stop them. But he'd failed. Barely. If Dad had found him first and been the one eaten . . . Maybe that had been the wolf's plan. He had expected the prince to find him and had only leapt on her because she'd discovered him. If she hadn't found him first . . . He could have killed them both.

The voices were coming closer.

The duffel bag lay where she'd dropped it. Picking it up, Dad strode to the curtains, threw them back, and raised the window. He took out the broomstick for himself and held out the bath mat to Julie. She unrolled it and climbed on.

Following her father, Julie flew out the window and over the crowd of tourists, reporters, and police. She didn't look down, and when Dad saw the trail of thorns again leading toward the setting sun, she didn't argue. She just flew.

## Chapter Ten
## *The Wild West*

They flew west.

One by one, stars poked through the sky, and the hills below washed out to gray. She barely noticed. Little Red Riding Hood's wolf had swallowed a girl, and a hero had sliced the wolf's stomach open to save her. Most likely, the Wild had swallowed Julie's house.

Oh, who was she kidding? Dad had chopped thorns, fit a glass slipper on a woman, and now killed Little Red's wolf. The Wild had to have swallowed all of Northboro by now.

At least this time, everyone would have recognized the danger. They would have evacuated instantly. She pictured the roads clogged with cars and hoped that Gillian had gotten out.

Mom and Grandma, trapped as pumpkins, wouldn't have been able to escape, she thought. No one would have known to save them. Jack, Gina, and their friends were the only people Julie had told about the pumpkin spell, and they'd been arrested. In saving Julie, Dad had condemned Mom and Grandma. If Julie hadn't walked into that room, if she had seen the wolf sooner, if she had run faster . . . Julie felt sick. The Wild was free, and Mom and Grandma were trapped inside—and this time, it really was her fault.

Below, the dark hills changed into thick patches of lights. Over the edge of the bath mat, she watched the lights of Little Rock, Arkansas, flash by. There were more than a hundred thousand people below. Did they know that the Wild was free again? Were they watching it on the news? Were they scared? She wondered if Bobbi knew that her plan had backfired—the wolf had failed, and worse, the Wild had been strengthened.

What could the fairy godmother possibly want with Sleeping Beauty that was worth the risk of the Wild escaping? What did she want that was worth killing or dying for? Jack was wrong—it wasn't a practical joke. It was serious. Deadly serious. And Julie and Dad were the only ones who knew. If Dad hadn't chased after Bobbi in the first place . . . "You were right all along," Julie said out loud. "Rose is in danger. How did you know?"

Dad was silent. Maybe he hadn't heard her over the wind. His eyes were still fixed on the thorns that threaded across Arkansas. "I did not know," he said at last. "But I had no other way to show my worth to Rapunzel. Or to you."

He didn't know? And he'd chased after Sleeping Beauty anyway? "You left Mom *as a pumpkin* in order to impress us?"

"In hindsight, it was perhaps not a well-thought-out choice."

"And you tried to leave me in New York too," she said. "That's twice."

"I feared for your safety," he said. Glancing at her, he added mildly, "It was not an unwarranted fear. You were eaten."

She shuddered, trying not to remember how it had felt to slide through the hot, wet, putrid jaws of the wolf. "What if you'd been wrong? You risked a lot. You don't know this world. Before yesterday, you'd never seen a car or an elevator—"

"It is not the difference in transportation or entertainment or homes or clothing that is difficult," he said. "It is the difference in the people I once knew."

She studied him as he flew. "You mean Mom."

He didn't answer and didn't look at her. His knuckles were white as he gripped the broomstick. His face was hidden in shadows.

Maybe Mom had changed. How was Julie to know? She hadn't known Mom five hundred years ago. "She could be the same inside," Julie said. "You didn't stay long enough to tell. You ran at the first opportunity."

"Yes, I know," he said.

"You *knew?*" And he'd done it anyway? He had no evidence that Rose's kidnapping was for real, yet he'd risked everything to chase her?

"Only in retrospect."

"If you had to do it over again, would you do today differently? Would you listen to Mom and Grandma and let them teach you how to fit into the world before plunging into it?"

He thought for a moment. "No," he said finally. "I am who I am."

She didn't know what to say to that. In silence, Julie and Dad flew on, leaving Arkansas behind them. Below, dark fields were covered in shadows, punctuated by scattered house lights and minuscule towns. It was nearly impossible to see the thorns left by Sleeping Beauty. As it grew darker, Dad and Julie slowed, matching the speed of trucks on the highway in order to see the thorns in their headlights. Julie began to shiver in the night chill. She wished she'd taken one of Elvis's coats. Her own had been pretty much ruined. She shivered harder and wished she could stop thinking about the wolf. Twice, she opened her mouth to talk to Dad and then shut it, unsure how to begin.

Somewhere over Oklahoma, Dad broke the silence. "Tell me about your mother. What is she like now?"

And so Julie began to talk. She told him little things

like Mom's favorite food (pizza with extra cheese and mush-rooms), medium things (one time, Mom locked herself out of the house and actually climbed down the chimney to get back in—a trick not recommended by the Three Little Pigs), and big things (Mom never, ever broke a promise that she made to Julie). When she ran out of things to say, it was late. Maybe close to midnight, Julie thought.

Back in Northboro, the pumpkin spell would be end-ing soon. Mom and Grandma would transform and find themselves trapped inside the Wild again. Julie had never meant for that to happen. She hadn't intended to aban-don them. It hadn't been a conscious choice, unlike when she'd chosen to walk through the door to the Wishing Well Motel . . . Inside a castle, she'd found a magic door that led directly to Grandma's motel. She knew if she opened that door, she'd lose her father. But if she didn't . . . "Dad . . . that afternoon in the Wild . . ." Standing at the motel door, she had made the decision to leave him in the Wild. She had chosen to leave him to what could have been centuries more of imprisonment and instead made a wish that set her hometown free. How did you say "sorry" for that? Did he understand why she had left him and walked through that door? Could he forgive her for it? She didn't even know how to ask.

He was silent. Julie couldn't read his expression in the dark. "You gave me great joy that day," he said finally.

Really? Despite everything, Julie smiled.

"But you have given me greater joy today," he said. "I never thought that I would have the opportunity to quest alongside my own child."

She'd never expected today either.

They continued to talk as they flew. Somewhere in western Oklahoma, when Julie grew so tired that her bath mat began to dip, they stopped to sleep. Julie's bath mat became her bed; Dad slept on the bare ground. Julie dreamt that her mother was in a tower, and she kept brushing her hair and humming as Julie called and called to her.

In the morning, Dad waltzed into a Dairy Queen. She didn't try to stop him. Who cared what some kid at the counter thought of him? The Wild was growing. Mom and Grandma were trapped inside it. The wolf was dead, and Sleeping Beauty was in danger. The normal rules didn't seem relevant anymore.

How had her world turned upside down so quickly? Just yesterday, the Wild had been subdued enough to become the topic of an English assignment. Julie drew the tattered pages of Gillian's English assignment out of her pocket. This was a memento now. While she waited for Dad, she read it.

The assignment had been to write about what had happened when Northboro was transformed into a fairy-tale kingdom, and so Gillian had written about the Wild. Sort of. As Julie read further, she realized that Gillian's Wild was utterly unlike the real Wild. In Gillian's story, you could be a princess or a knight or even a witch, but the Wild didn't control your actions. You had a choice about what to do, and you knew who you were. The Wild didn't force you into a story, and you didn't lose your memories. In Gillian's story, being in the Wild was fun. In her story, the Wild was *nice*.

Gillian had promised to lie to protect Julie's family, but this . . . this was taking it too far. She'd practically glorified the Wild. How could she do that? How could she even imagine that there was anything good about the Wild? Gillian had been forced to play a magic trumpet while trolls and bears and other wild animals danced for hours and hours, until her lips were so sore that she could barely speak. How could she romanticize the Wild after living through that?

Dad emerged from the Dairy Queen with three paper bags. "I was victorious," he said, smiling broadly.

Ooh, were those cheeseburgers? Please say they were cheeseburgers. Story forgotten, Julie shoved the pages back into her pocket and took a bag. Yes! Double cheeseburger!

The Dairy Queen door banged open, and a teenage girl scurried out with two more white bags. "Here!" she said, shoving them at Prince. "Fries!" She giggled and then ran back inside, but not before Julie glimpsed her T-shirt. Rhinestone letters read, Princess in Disguise.

"What did you say to her?" Julie asked. She shoved a handful of fries into her mouth. Mmm, salt. It had been a long time since the last vending machine.

"I told her that her happily-ever-after would come," he said, climbing onto his broomstick. "She seemed to like that."

Suddenly, the fries tasted like dust in her mouth. She thought of Gillian's story. She thought of the tourists at Graceland. What if, instead of fleeing from the Wild, people actually flocked in? What if they believed that the Wild would turn them into princes and princesses, give them happily-ever-afters, and make their dreams come true? Higgins Armory Museum in Worcester had apparently been flooded with visitors ever since it had transformed into the Castle of the Silver Towers. She'd seen people at school in tiaras, and of course there were those Fairy-Tale Capital T-shirts and bumper stickers and signs.

What if people were making it worse?

"Did she say anything about how far the Wild has spread?" Julie asked, trying to keep her voice from shaking.

"She did not," Prince said, "but she, in her innocence, is eager for it to come. She spoke of it as if it were a traveling carnival, as if she would spend one day inside the Wild, enjoy its stories, and then resume her normal life."

Oh, no. If people everywhere thought like that . . . if they were actually entering the Wild instead of running from it . . . then it could have grown even more than Julie had feared. It could have spread across all of Massachusetts. Julie shuddered and hoped she was wrong.

\* \* \*

Flying at twice the speed of cars, Julie and Prince caught up with the thorns again outside of Amarillo, Texas. In the late afternoon, in Arizona, the trail turned onto a smaller road and headed north. Julie and Dad turned north too, skimming over the road with the thorns directly in front of them.

At sunset, they reached the Grand Canyon.

Julie and Dad flew over red rock hills as the sun touched the horizon. Up ahead, light spread across the canyon walls, and the rocks seemed to burst into deep red flame. "Whoa," Julie breathed. She'd seen photos. But the reality . . . It was beyond vast. Even from the sky, she couldn't see all of the canyon at once. Clinging to the edge of the bath mat, she felt dizzy.

"Up!" Dad shouted.

Startled, Julie yanked the front fringe up. The bottom of her bath mat grazed the roof of an RV. She sailed up over it. Her heart thudded faster as she joined Dad circling above the camper. She'd been so distracted by the canyon that she'd failed to see the RV parked directly in their path.

Just a few yards beyond the RV, the road terminated in a picnic area and the canyon began. "The thorns end here,"

Dad said. He pointed at a line of brambles that ran up to and underneath the RV.

Was Sleeping Beauty in there? But . . . why an RV, and why the rim of the Grand Canyon? Why had Bobbi brought her to another tourist spot?

"Stay in the air," Dad said. "It may be a trap." He drew his sword.

Julie had a sudden image of Dad charging in on a family of innocent tourists. "We don't know for sure it's them," she said. Had Bobbi really traded the apple coach for an RV? She didn't seem the RV type. "If Sleeping Beauty really is inside, shouldn't there be more thorns?" The RV was parked. Thorns should be crawling up its wheels. It should be half cocooned in brambles at least. "Maybe the trail picks up somewhere else."

Dad hesitated.

Below, the RV door swung open. A boy leaned outside and dumped soda from an open can onto the ground. He didn't look up. He didn't see them. But Julie saw his face as he turned back inside.

It was the boy from Graceland, the Cutest Boy Ever, Henry.

She felt her heart skip a beat. How could it be him? It couldn't be him. He couldn't have gotten here before Julie and Prince . . . unless he and his dad had left Graceland immediately and driven for, like, twenty hours straight.

Henry *had* said that they planned to visit Graceland, the Grand Canyon, and Disneyland. Maybe this was a coincidence. And maybe it was also a coincidence that of all the spots to park at the Grand Canyon, Henry and his dad happened to choose the end of the trail of thorns. A very, very big coincidence.

But what if it wasn't? Dad had mistaken Henry's father for Rumpelstiltskin and Julie had assumed he was wrong. What if he wasn't? The run-in with the wolf proved that other fairy-tale characters were involved in Sleeping Beauty's kidnapping. "What if Sleeping Beauty isn't with Bobbi anymore?" she said. "What if Bobbi handed her off to someone else?" They knew Bobbi had changed her mode of transportation since she'd ditched the apple coach back in New York City. What if she'd loaded Sleeping Beauty into Rumpelstiltskin's RV?

Dad brandished his sword in the air. "We shall demand entry and search for her!"

On the other hand, what if this was a huge mistake? "What if they're innocent?" Julie asked. "Maybe we should . . . I don't know . . . be sneaky or something."

"Do you have a plan?" Dad asked.

Um . . . no, not really. But Julie loved that he was asking her. Before the wolf, he would have simply charged in without waiting for her. Now they were like a team. The RV door opened again, and this time Henry's dad (could he be Rumpelstiltskin?) stepped out of the camper. Slinging a garbage bag over his shoulder like he was Santa Claus, he proceeded to cart it down the road toward a public trash can. "If you can keep him away from the RV for a few minutes, I can try to convince Henry to let me inside," Julie said to Dad. "I can be like a spy."

He nodded. "It is a good plan. You are your mother's daughter."

Well, it wasn't a save-the-world sort of plan, and it had the potential to be mind-bogglingly humiliating, but it was (moderately) better than charging in, sword raised. "And my father's daughter too," she said.

He smiled at her, and Julie felt as if sun had burst through the clouds. Drawing courage from his smile, she flew down to the RV and hopped off the bath mat. Before she could reconsider, she knocked.

Henry opened the door. "Hey, I know you! You were at Graceland! Julie, right?" He remembered her! Wait, was that because he liked her or because he was part of some nefarious plot? Or was it because he was just friendly? Friendly *and* cute?

"Um, hi," Julie stammered. "Um, sorry to bother you." How do you phrase *I think you have Sleeping Beauty in your RV*? She wished she'd thought this out for maybe three seconds before she knocked, especially now that Henry was smiling at her. He had a really, really nice smile. "Um, this is going to sound a little crazy . . ." Or maybe a lot crazy.

"Like calling-my-dad-Rumpelstiltskin crazy?"

Yeah, a lot like that kind of crazy. "Like thorns-covering-Graceland crazy."

He thought about it for a second. "Okay."

In a single breath, Julie said, "I think you might have a woman in your RV, a sleeping woman, like comatose-sleeping, with, uh, thorns and stuff around her."

He blinked. "Huh?"

"Um, it's possible that, ahh, um . . . Sleeping Beauty is in your RV," she said. She felt her face turn scarlet.

Henry stared at her. "Uh, I told you before, it's just my dad and me. I think I would have noticed if we'd picked up a thorny sleeping woman."

He so thought she was crazy. Great. Still blushing furiously, she said, "Listen, I know this is a weird request, but can I just look around your RV? Really quick. Please?" Oh, God, this was sooo embarrassing.

His green eyes widened. "Is that a bath mat? Is it *floating*? Wow, that is so cool!" He shot her a look of total admiration, which made her blush even more. As he stepped outside to stare at the bath mat, she caught a glimpse of a table inside the RV. On the table was a canister of weed killer. She felt the blood drain out of her cheeks. *Weed killer.*

No wonder there weren't more thorns around the RV.

"You do have her!" Julie charged inside, and Henry

flattened against the side of the camper as the floating bath mat trailed behind her.

She sped through the RV. Closet-like bathroom, no. Cabinets, no. Under the table, no. Bed, no. Where could you hide a grown woman in a camper? She dove for the cushions on the couch and tossed them over her shoulder.

"Hey!" Henry said. "What are you doing? You're making a mess. Dad is going to flip his lid. I don't think I should have let you inside. Who are you? And where did you get that bath mat? It's awesome!"

She paused. He thought it was awesome? He was looking at her. Wow, he had movie-star eyes. Julie forced herself to look back down at the couch. Cushions aside, she saw a handle. Yes! She was right! "Look!" she said, pointing. A hidden compartment! Did he doubt her now?

"All RVs have extra storage there," he said. "We don't keep anything in it. Well, we were going to pack camping gear—hey!" he said as Julie yanked up the lid . . .

. . . and saw blankets.

The RV door banged open. "Henry, are you okay?" called his father. *Was* he Rumpelstiltskin? Maybe he wasn't. What if she was wrong? But there was the weed killer and . . . Okay, there was no real other evidence, but it *couldn't* be just a coincidence. She refused to believe it was just a co-incidence.

Dad charged into the RV. "Halt!" he cried as Henry's

dad tried to grab her arm. Julie yanked back the blankets.

Everyone froze.

"Whoa," Henry said.

Sleeping Beauty lay in the storage compartment with arms crossed as if she were in a coffin. Butter yellow hair framed her pink-cheeked face. She was alive, breathing softly and delicately.

Dad leveled his sword at Rumpelstiltskin's throat. "Your evil plan has been thwarted." The tip touched skin. Julie remembered red on gray fur and shouted, "Dad, no!" He'd do it, she thought wildly. He was a hero; heroes slayed villains. She rushed to his side.

"Evil plan thwarted? Who talks like that?" Henry said, his voice shrill and fast. "Dad, what's going on? Who are these people? Is that a real sword? Why's that dude dressed like Elvis?"

Julie clung to Dad's arm. "Dad, please."

The prince didn't lower the sword. "Explain to your son what evil you have wrought."

"Who's that woman?" Henry asked, voice still shrill. "Is she . . . She couldn't be. She's *not* Sleeping Beauty. That's impossible."

Defying the prince, Rumpelstiltskin lifted his chin, exposing more of his throat to the sword point. "Please, please, don't," Julie begged Dad. He'd already killed once for her. "I'm safe. Sleeping Beauty's safe."

He didn't look at her. The sword didn't waver.

"Do what you will to me," Rumpelstiltskin said, "but leave my son. He's innocent." His eyes flickered to Henry. "I had no choice," he said quietly. "They threatened you. I would ransom the world to protect you."

Yes, of course, Julie realized. He was Rumpelstiltskin. He had bargained with a miller's daughter for her baby, and then he had torn himself in two with anger and grief when he hadn't been able to win the child. Of all the fairy-tale characters, he was the one who had wanted a child the most. He was the one who had been willing to go the farthest to have one. Now that he had a son, he would of course do anything for him. Bobbi must have known that.

Dad knew it too. He lowered his sword.

"All I had to do in return for my son's safety was transport Sleeping Beauty. I was allowed to choose the route, so I disguised the journey as a vacation."

Julie finally understood. That was why Sleeping Beauty was at Graceland and here at the Grand Canyon! Her path had been disguised as an ordinary road trip for Henry's sake.

"You weren't supposed to ever know," Rumpelstiltskin said to his son. "If I obeyed my orders, you'd be left alone. You wouldn't be harmed."

Eyes wild, Henry looked from his dad to Julie to Prince. "This is crazy!"

Julie tried to imagine what he was feeling. It had been tough enough to grow up knowing her family's secret, but how much worse would it have been to discover that her mom had been hiding the truth all along? "What kind of threats did Bobbi make?" Julie asked. She pictured Henry as a pumpkin. Was that really enough of a threat to get involved in a kidnapping? Wasn't Rumpelstiltskin risking his son by involving him at all?

"Oh, Bobbi's not the dangerous one," said Rumpelstiltskin. "She's bad, but the one she works for . . ." He shuddered. Wait—what did he mean? There was someone *worse* than a rogue fairy godmother? Bobbi had a boss?

Henry shook his head as if trying to shake the words out of his ears. "You expect me to believe . . . Are you saying . . . You're *really* Rumpelstiltskin?"

Julie shivered. That sounded a lot like a fairy-tale moment: someone had guessed Rumpelstiltskin's true identity. Had they just fueled the Wild again? "He's still your dad before anything else," Julie said. "Nothing changes that."

Henry forced a laugh. "It's all a big joke, right?" He looked pleadingly at Julie and then he spun around, his eyes darting all over the RV. "Okay, where are the hidden cameras? Very funny. Hilarious." His voice cracked on the final word. Bending over Sleeping Beauty, he poked her shoulder. "Joke's over. You can get up now."

Julie wished she could say it was a joke. She wished she

could tell him it would all be okay. This was such a terrible way for someone to find out the truth.

"Sleeping Beauty will sleep until awakened by a kiss," Dad said. He laid the broomstick and duffel bag on the counter behind him and pushed past Rumpelstiltskin.

Julie scooted between her dad and Sleeping Beauty. "You know you can't kiss her, right?"

"I do not wish to be faithless to your mother or to what she believes is right," he said, "but the spell must be broken. It would be cruel to leave Rose asleep for longer than is needed. Sleeping through life . . . it is the one of the cruelest fates within the Wild." Gently, he pushed Julie aside.

Behind him, Rumpelstiltskin said, "If you kiss her, you'll fuel the Wild."

Julie nodded vigorously. See! Even the villains knew that was bad.

He added: "You'll be playing right into their hands."

Both Julie and Prince turned to stare at him. "What?" Julie said, stunned. Someone *wanted* Dad to wake Sleeping Beauty? Someone *wanted* the Wild to grow faster? She had to have misheard.

"The kiss was supposed to take place in Sleeping Beauty's castle in Disneyland for maximum fairy-tale impact of setting plus characters," Rumpelstiltskin explained. An actual prince waking an actual princess inside a castle . . . Yes, that would have given the Wild an incredible burst of strength.

"Are you saying this whole mess isn't about Sleeping Beauty at all?" Julie asked. "This is about the Wild? About *helping* the Wild?" But that couldn't be! No fairy-tale character would ever want to help the Wild . . . would they?

It was totally and utterly inconceivable. But the pieces fit:

1. Bobbi's strange behavior. As Cinderella's fairy godmother, Bobbi could poof herself from place to place, yet she had chosen to flee Worcester in a highly visible apple coach. She had transformed Mom and Grandma into pumpkins but not Dad. In fact, Bobbi had dared Dad to chase her. She knew if she kidnapped Sleeping Beauty right there in front of an actual prince, he wouldn't be able to resist, and then she'd have a prince on a quest to save a princess.

2. The glass slipper in Times Square. Could Bobbi have planted the glass slipper deliberately? Maybe she was the one who had egged on the crowd! Or what if it had been someone else, like this "boss" that Rumpelstiltskin had mentioned . . .

3. The birds. The pigeons that attacked . . . they could have been under orders to re-create a fairy-tale event. Later, they could have pointed the way to the trail of thorns.

4. Jack and Gina's arrest. The police had mentioned an informant—could it have been Bobbi's boss or some other fairy-tale character who wanted to keep Jack and Gina and the others from stopping Dad?

5. The wolf. After New York, Bobbi must have transferred Sleeping Beauty to Rumpelstiltskin, who then left on his "spontaneous" road trip with Henry, leading Julie and the prince to Graceland, where the wolf . . . Julie shivered. Oh, wow. She'd thought that at worst, this was about one reckless kidnapping. She never imagined there could be a conspiracy! "You're working *for* the Wild?" Julie demanded.

He held up his hands in defense. "I was only transportation!"

"Only transportation?" She gawked at him. He was the one with Sleeping Beauty in his RV. He was the one who laid the trail that led them to the wolf! "How about 'kidnapping' and 'attempted murder'?" Her voice cracked, and she realized she'd been shouting.

"Murder?" Henry yelped.

Rumpelstiltskin crumpled against the wall of the RV as Julie told him about the wolf. Henry backed away from both of them as she talked.

"I didn't know." Rumpelstiltskin pleaded to Henry, "I swear I didn't know."

Henry turned away from his dad and stared out the window at the canyon. Julie saw him wipe a cheek with the back of his fist. Later, she promised herself, she'd talk to him. She'd *finally* met another kid whose parent was a fairy-tale character! They had a lot to talk about—if he was ever willing to speak to her again.

In a whisper, Rumpelstiltskin said, "Tell me how I can make it better."

He couldn't, she thought. The wolf was dead. The Wild was growing. And Sleeping Beauty . . . "You can wake Sleeping Beauty!" Julie exclaimed. Yes, that was perfect! "It's not a fairy-tale moment if the villain kisses her, right?" They could wreck the kidnappers' plans right here!

"I . . . suppose it's not," Rumpelstiltskin said.

"He's not a prince," Dad objected. "It may not work. She might not wake."

Still facing the window, Henry gave a choked laugh. This all had to feel like a nightmare to him. His world was turning upside down. But Julie couldn't think about him right now. Pay attention, she told herself. You can stop the kidnappers' plan right here. "Just try it," she said to Rumpelstiltskin. "Please."

Rumpelstiltskin knelt by Sleeping Beauty. Julie held her breath. Would it work? Dad was right; Rumpelstiltskin wasn't a prince. What if it didn't work?

Henry interrupted, his voice even more strained, "Uh . . . 'Scuze me? Which one of you brought the dragon?"

Julie turned, and her stomach lurched. Out the window, a dragon—its wings spread radiantly against the dying sun—rose out of the Grand Canyon.

## Chapter Eleven
### *The Dragon*

"Get down!" Rumpelstiltskin leapt onto his son, knocking him to the floor. Julie fell to her knees as her dad shielded her. She saw a flash of iridescent scales and silver claws as the dragon dove for the window and then veered up.

Metal crunched, and then rosy sunlight poured in as the roof of the RV was peeled back like the lid on a can of cat food. Julie screamed as wind from the dragon's wings rushed into the camper, and then the dragon's shadow fell over them.

Dad drew his sword.

"It's the next trap!" Rumpelstiltskin shouted. "They want a prince to fight a dragon!"

"Don't fight it, Dad!" She grabbed his sword arm.

The dragon plunged its claws deep into the camper. One set of talons closed around Rumpelstiltskin and Henry. The other scooped up Sleeping Beauty.

Julie released Dad's arm and shrieked. "Never mind! Fight it, Dad! Fight it!"

Wind whooshed into the camper again as the dragon took flight. As its shadow lifted, the rose red sunset glinted off Dad's sword. "Leave them and fight me!" Dad cried to the dragon. He jumped onto his broomstick and shot up out of the torn-open roof of the RV.

Grabbing her bath mat, Julie flew up after him and then stopped, hovering above the RV. A few yards ahead, the earth dropped away in a mammoth cliff. She watched the dragon soar out over the Grand Canyon. Behind it, the sun was nearly down. The dragon spread its wings, and its translucent skin glowed like sheets of gold. The scales on its body flashed red, gold, and emerald. She saw its prisoners as dark shapes. Sleeping Beauty hung limp from her waist, and Henry and Rumpelstiltskin struggled in the dragon's talons, a mile above the Grand Canyon.

Sword raised high, Dad dove at the dragon.

The dragon twisted away from him. Silhouetted against the dark blue sky, Julie watched in horror as the dragon opened its jaws, and a jet of fire blazed across the sky.

Fire-breathing dragon! "Dad, watch out!" she screamed.

Dad jerked to the left, and the fire blasted past him, missing him by inches.

The dragon shot another burst of flame at Dad, and its prisoners screamed. Dad spiraled away and dove toward the dragon's back, causing it to twist in mid-air and shoot another stream of fire at Dad. Stripes of smoke filled the air, drifting into darkened clouds. He would never get close enough to strike!

What should Julie do? What *could* she do? She didn't have a sword. She didn't even have a butter knife. She just had herself and a stupid flying bath mat . . . I could distract the dragon, she thought suddenly. I could get its attention, and Dad could strike!

Taking a deep breath, Julie leaned forward on the bath mat and flew out over the canyon. Her stomach dropped as the earth fell away beneath her. Don't look down, she thought. Just don't look down.

"Hey, dragon!" she shouted. "Over here!"

"Julie, stay back!" Dad yelled.

The dragon swung its head toward her. Behind it, the sun was now a sliver of orange-red as bright as the dragon's fire. She swallowed hard. "That's it! Watch me, you overgrown gecko!"

She heard Henry cry, "What are you *doing?*"

As the dragon opened its jaws, Julie dove down, faster, faster—the wind whipping through her hair. A mile below, she saw the Colorado River like a strip of black ribbon. She aimed straight for it.

Wind rushed behind her, and she shot a look back. Oh, no, the dragon wasn't supposed to follow her! She was only supposed to be a momentary distraction. It wasn't supposed to start chasing her! Julie saw its jaws open. Instinctively, she yanked up on the bath mat. She heard the air crackle, and a jet of flame burned through the air right where she had just been. Faster, she ordered herself. Faster!

Julie swooped through the canyons. Up, down, right, left. She circled around pillars of rock as thick and tall as skyscrapers. She skirted along jagged ridges.

The dragon kept coming.

She had to find someplace where the dragon couldn't follow. But where? The sun was gone now. Only the deep orange afterglow remained. Shadows filled the impossibly wide canyons. Could she hide down there? Maybe if she flew fast enough, she could escape into the darkness. Pointing the bath mat down, she dove. She gritted her teeth as wind slapped her face. She shot a look over her shoulder and saw the dragon diving after her like a torpedo. Its wings were tucked into its sides, and its talons holding Henry, Rumpelstiltskin, and Sleeping Beauty were pulled up against its chest. "Faster! Faster!" she shouted at the bath mat.

She plunged deep into the canyon. As the canyon walls blurred on either side of her, she saw the river below. In the shadows, it looked like a road of black glass. On either side, Julie saw trees. She could hide there! Surely, the dragon was too huge to follow her between them. As she dove closer, she yanked up on the front fringe and glided over the top branches of a patch of trees. "Slower, slower," she whispered to the mat. She skimmed over branches, slowing. As soon as she was slow enough, she'd—

"Julie!" her dad yelled. Henry and Rumpelstiltskin yelled too.

She turned her head. Red fire shot toward her, so bright and close that for an instant, it was all she could see. Without thinking, Julie rolled off the bath mat. She landed hard in a cradle of branches. Air squeezed out of her lungs. The bath mat zipped past her and then burst into flames. A small fireball, it hurtled toward the canyon wall and slammed into the rocks in a shower of sparks.

Her body aching in a thousand places, Julie clutched at branches as the sparks faded and the canyon floor finally fell into shadows. The afterimages of the fireball danced in front of her eyes and, for a moment, Julie couldn't see anything. She heard the whoosh-whoosh of wind from the dragon's wings, and she held her breath. If she couldn't see it, could it see her?

"Julie!" her dad called. "Answer me, Julie! Are you all right?"

"Julie!" Henry shouted at the same time.

If she called back to them, would she reveal herself to the dragon? If she didn't—She saw a streak of fire blaze across the sky high above her. Against its glow, she saw the silhouette of her father, directly in the fire's path. "Dad, watch out!"

"Julie!" Dad dove toward her.

The dragon flew to intercept him.

She screamed as the dragon's head turned toward Dad. It was too close! Dad wouldn't be able to—

Suddenly, in a deep, echoing voice, the dragon spoke: "Prince!" *What?* The dragon talked! Its voice reverberated across the canyon. "We have your beloved!" Your beloved? *Mom?* The kidnappers had Mom? A jet of flame sizzled through the air right between Dad and Julie. In that blaze of light, Julie saw the dragon. It was directly over her head! If it looked down, it would see her!

As the dragon's fire faded, it vanished again into shadows.

"My master waits for you!" the dragon cried in the darkness. "She holds your Rapunzel! If you want to save your love, you must complete your quest! Come to the castle!" Julie heard the whoosh of wings, and she saw the shadow of the dragon rise out of the canyon toward the deep blue sky. Stars pierced through the blue, and the dragon was nothing more than a black shadow in the distance.

"Dad?" Julie called. Where was he? She heard Henry and Rumpelstiltskin both shouting from far away, but she couldn't make out the words.

"Do not worry!" Dad called to Julie. "I will save her! I will save them all!"

Oh, no, he couldn't be planning to chase after them! "Dad, it's a trap!" Julie yelled. She saw his silhouette against the blue sky as he flew upward. No, no, no, he had to rescue Julie first! "Take me with you! Dad, no!"

She couldn't chase him. She'd lost the bath mat. She didn't have any tricks up her sleeve . . . Wait, yes, she did. Jack's magic beans! She still had the bottle from Jack's medicine cabinet. If it grew fast enough, she could climb the beanstalk and meet Dad in the sky! Julie yanked the bottle out, pulled off the cover, and shook out a single bean. The bean fell through the branches of the tree.

For one endless second, there was silence.

Julie heard rumbling. Looking down, she saw one of the shadows move. In seconds, it fired past her, a thickening stalk. Leaves burst from its sides. Julie took a deep breath and jumped from her nest of branches onto the beanstalk. She wrapped her arms and legs around it and held on, riding the beanstalk up as it blasted faster and faster skyward from the floor of the Grand Canyon.

"Dad!" she called as the beanstalk cleared the rim. In the distance, she saw the small shadow that was Dad, chasing the dragon. "Dad, come back!"

He didn't slow, and the beanstalk kept growing. With Julie clinging to its top, the beanstalk plunged up into the dark blue night.

## Chapter Twelve
### *The Closet*

Coughing and hacking, Zel woke. She lay cheek-down in a puddle of drool. She recoiled from it. What had—

Linda. Apple. *Poison.*

In her tale, Snow White had woken up after the poisoned apple was dislodged from her throat; a similar thing must have happened to Zel. Her stomach must have rejected the poison, causing her to wake.

She took a deep, long breath and sat up. Wiping her cheek and grimacing, Zel looked around her. No dwarves this time. She was alone in what looked like a closet. Empty shelves lined the walls. On one end was a small stained glass window (odd choice for a closet window, she thought) and on the other was a door.

Zel went to the door and laid her ear against it. She heard voices. Linda, maybe? The sounds were too muffled for her to be certain. Quietly, she tried the doorknob. Locked, of course. She'd need to find another way out—and then make her way home, find Julie, and stop the Wild.

Zel was not, not, not going to think about Julie in the Wild. She had to be somewhere else. She had to be safe. Prince had to be looking out for her. All Zel needed to do was escape and join them.

Prince *would* look after Julie, wouldn't he? He was her father. Not that he'd had any practice being a father. He was, in fact, a stranger to Julie. As much as she hated to admit it, he was a stranger to Zel too. It had been five hundred years since she'd seen him or spoken with him. She was trusting her daughter's safety to a man she remembered more as a dream than as a reality.

Zel crossed to the window. The stained glass depicted a ruby red rose against a deep blue sky. Stepping on a shelf, she tried to see outside. The red glass obscured the view. Where had Linda taken her? Zel squinted and tried a different angle. Through a pane of blue glass, she thought she saw the shape of horses, frozen in mid-step. As she watched, the horses began to move . . . A carousel? Could this be some kind of amusement park?

That meant there *had* to be people outside. Zel could call for help! If she could pop a pane of glass out, then maybe she could shout loud enough for someone to hear before her captors could stop her. Yes! She had a plan!

Zel began to push at one of the panes. Why would Linda

bring her to an amusement park, of all places? Why would Linda bring her anywhere? Who *was* Linda?

As she worked on the window pane, Zel ran through the list of possible fairy-tale villains. Clearly, Linda couldn't be Snow White's evil stepmother. She had mentioned that the queen had provided her disguise; Linda wouldn't have said that if she actually was the queen. She also couldn't be Cinderella's stepmother—Zel had met her, and there was no way she could have hidden her ego for so many years. Linda wasn't likely to be any of the stepsisters either—they had both moved on and now had lives of their own. Zel would have heard if any of them had suddenly left their homes and families. Linda had to be someone that Zel had lost track of . . . like Sleeping Beauty's evil fairy.

The more she thought about it, the more obvious the answer became. Of course! Linda *had* to be the evil fairy from Sleeping Beauty's tale. The evil fairy was the only villain with a personal connection to Rose. Plus, Zel hadn't run into her in at least a century.

Zel wished now that she had kept better track of all the other fairy-tale characters. She knew the ones who visited or lived in Northboro, but there were scores of characters that had drifted away. She wished she'd made the effort to keep in touch with everyone. Maybe then Linda wouldn't have been able to surprise her.

Zel replayed the events on top of the car. She should

never have turned her back on Linda. You don't turn your back on an enemy. But she hadn't ever imagined that Linda could be dangerous. She'd known Linda as the children's room librarian for years! She'd helped four-year-old Julie get her first library card. She'd come into the salon for a trim every two months. She'd always been a little excitable, a little more passionate about books than your average person, but she was supposed to be—she was a librarian, after all. Zel had long ago placed her in the "harmless" category in her mind. How could she have been so wrong? How could she not have guessed that Linda was a fairy-tale character too? Yes, Linda had disguised herself, but there *must* have been clues. No one could change all their mannerisms. No one could hide who they really were all the time. But Linda had faked normal well. She'd fooled everyone.

And she was still fooling people. So far, only Zel knew that Linda was the evil fairy. I have to get out, Zel thought. I have to warn everyone!

With one final push, a chunk of blue glass popped out of the window, tumbled down toward the moat, and splashed into the water. She heard a squawk and more splashing as ducks scattered below. Pressing her face against the hole, Zel shouted, "Help! Call 911! I've been kidnapped! I'm trapped in a closet! Please help!"

She heard a soft pop behind her.

Oh, no.

Zel glanced around quickly for something, anything, to defend herself with but saw nothing. She turned. Glitter hung in the air around Cinderella's fairy godmother. Bobbi's pink poofed skirt filled half the closet. She looked as if she'd stepped out of a storybook illustration. Zel felt queasy; she hadn't seen Bobbi look like that in centuries. Zel had a bad, bad feeling about this.

"So sorry, Zel," Bobbi said. "Your prince isn't here to rescue you. Yet." She waved a roll of duct tape in the air. "Until then, I've been instructed to keep you quiet."

Yet? What did she mean "yet"? "Where is he?" Zel demanded. "And where's Julie? What have you done with them?"

"Oh, we haven't done anything." Bobbi smirked. "Your prince has done it all of his own free will." She giggled. "He fit a glass slipper on a Cinderella wannabe, he cut a girl out of the belly of a wolf, he fought a dragon who had kidnapped a princess . . ."

With each word, Zel's heart sank lower. "What are you doing?" she whispered. Those were major fairy-tale moments!

Bobbi waved her wand, and a chair and a coil of rope appeared in front of her. "I'm tying you up," she said matter-of-factly, "so that you aren't tempted to pull the duct tape off or do something else unspeakably clever."

Zel felt sick. This was worse than a pumpkin spell, worse

than being poisoned, worse than anything she could imagine. "You're helping the Wild," she said flatly. "You want the Wild to return."

Bobbi reached forward and tweaked Zel's nose. "Bingo! Now sit in this chair and put your arms behind your back so I can tie you up like in the movies." She giggled, and her wings fluttered. "Alternately, I could turn you into a pumpkin again. Or maybe you'd prefer to be a frog?" She'd do it, Zel thought. She could see it in the fairy godmother's dancing eyes. Bobbi wanted to do it.

Still looking for something, anything, that could be a weapon, Zel moved slowly over into the chair. "Fine. I'll sit." Don't antagonize the crazy woman with the magic wand. Was she crazy? Was the answer as simple as that? But if she *was* crazy, how had Bobbi hidden it so well? She'd seemed so helpful after the Wild. She'd stuck around instead of returning to Florida and helped gather up the leftover fairy-tale items strewn all over town. She'd disenchanted frogs and swan-men. She'd helped to muddy the trail that led to any real fairy-tale character. It had to be because of Linda. *She wants it back*, the third blind mouse had said. Linda was behind this. Linda was the boss. "Why are you doing this?" Zel asked. "You can't have forgotten what the Wild was like. Is Linda forcing you? What hold does she have over you?"

Bobbi wrapped the rope around Zel's wrists. "Oh, I had

forgotten," she said, "and then for the first time in five hundred years, I had a taste once more of what it means to be the fairy godmother." She yanked the ropes, and Zel bit back a yelp. "Linda promised that I could have that again. She had a plan, you see, a beautiful plan. And it's working perfectly, despite all of your daughter's attempts to interfere. I *told* Linda that she should let me pumpkinify her. Your daughter's a persistent little brat. A lot like you, actually. Both of you, so sure you know what's best for everyone. News flash: we're not all happy here."

Julie! What was Julie doing? Was she all right? "You're still the fairy godmother outside of the Wild," Zel said, trying to reason with Bobbi. She fought to keep her voice even. Maybe she could talk her way out of this. She had to focus, to think of a strategy. Her brain kept shouting: *Julie, Julie, Julie!*

Bobbi laughed without a shred of humor in her voice. "Outside the Wild, I'm retired. I hide my magic. I pretend that I am no one of import." She knotted the rope.

"But in the Wild, you'll forget your past," Zel said. I'll forget my past, Zel thought. I'll forget Julie. I can't, can't, can't. "You'll forget everything you've gained in the last five hundred years!"

Bobbi secured the final knot, and then she picked up the roll of duct tape.

"You'll forget you!" Zel cried.

"Oh, no, Zel, you're wrong," Bobbi said with a happy smile. "I'll finally *be* me." She tore off a strip of duct tape.

"Don't—" Zel began.

Bobbi placed the duct tape over Zel's mouth firmly. "Don't worry," she said. "We'll make sure your prince comes. And if your darling Julie tries to interfere again . . . Linda has plans for her too."

## Chapter Thirteen
### *Beanstalks*

The beanstalk pierced the clouds. Mist dampened Julie's cheeks, and everything disappeared into foggy gray. She couldn't hear anything but wind and . . . wait! Were those voices?

"Dad?" she called.

No answer. It couldn't be Dad. She'd seen him fly away, leaving her behind again. Julie swallowed a lump in her throat. She'd thought they'd grown closer. When he saved her from the wolf, she'd thought he really cared. How could he leave her, stranded in a tree at the bottom of the Grand Canyon with night approaching? What kind of father did that? What kind of hero? Her eyes blurred, and she felt a tear slip down her cheek. Fiercely, Julie wiped it away. Crying wouldn't make him come back. And it wouldn't keep him from flying into a trap or prevent the Wild from growing one leaf larger.

She heard more voices. They sounded as if they were coming from *above* her. How was that possible? She was at least a mile, maybe two, above the Grand Canyon. How did they get up here?

"Hello? Help!" she called. Gripping the leaves, she climbed higher until she poked through the clouds at the very top of the beanstalk. The tip curled into an S, crowned with a leaf. She clung to the tip and looked around her.

Low, across a field of soft clouds, Julie saw the moon, a crescent that bathed the sky and clouds in a blue-ivory glow. The sky was a rich dark blue speckled with stars. Behind her was a castle.

"Whoa," Julie breathed. A castle. Here. In the clouds.

She told herself that she shouldn't be surprised. After all, if Grandma's broomstick could fly in the real world, if Bobbi's wand could change people into pumpkins, and if the wishing well could grant wishes, then why shouldn't magic beans work too? And no matter where they were, magic beans always grew into beanstalks that reached the giant's castle in the clouds. But still, a castle over Arizona . . . wow.

The castle loomed over the skyscape like the shadow of a monster. Dark stone, it blotted out the stars. Blue-gray mist swirled around the base. Coming in and out of the castle, Julie saw the silhouettes of creatures from fairy tales:

bears, lions, unicorns, fairies, elves, a girl with a goat's head, a woman with a snake's tail.

Maybe they could help Julie find her parents! Maybe they'd have another enchanted bath mat. Or even just an enchanted towel . . .

"Hello!" Julie called. "Over here! Help!"

Wind whisked her words away. She was too far away for them to hear. Julie reached out a foot, expecting to feel something solid that she could stand on, but she felt nothing except slightly damp air. She wiggled her foot in the cloud. Still nothing. But . . . but . . . there was a castle! An enormous, very heavy stone castle! If the clouds could hold a castle, they had to be able to support her. Leaning away from the beanstalk, she reached her foot out as far as she could . . .

. . . and her toes touched softness. Yes! It felt like the soft wet ooze at the bottom of a pond. Gripping a leaf with one hand, she leaned. The cloud held. Taking a deep breath, she released the beanstalk and walked onto the clouds.

Julie grinned. Oh, wow, she was walking on clouds. Wait until she told Gillian. This was *exactly* the kind of thing that Gillian would love—the kind of thing that made her wear fairy-tale T-shirts and write stories about a nice, even *fun* version of the Wild. Julie's smile faded. After Dad fought the dragon, the Wild had to have grown even more. If Gillian hadn't fled far enough away . . . Or worse, if she hadn't fled at all . . .

By now, Gillian was probably experiencing how very *not* nice the Wild was. Which tale had she been trapped in? Had she already forgotten who she was? Did she think she was a stepsister or a neglected orphan or a young girl lost in the woods?

The moon lit Julie's way across the clouds as she walked toward the castle. She hoped some of the creatures were friendly. So far, she hadn't seen any that she knew, though it was hard to tell at this distance. She did recognize some (the half-dragon woman, the hedgehog boy, the trolls) from their stories, but she'd never met them—which was strange, she thought, since as Gillian's T-shirt said, her hometown was the fairy-tale capital of the world, whether people knew it or not. Who were they and why hadn't they ever come to Northboro? Had they ever left these clouds? Why were they here? She imagined finding another prince, one who could catch Dad, rescue Mom and the others, and defeat the kidnappers. And, of course, stop the Wild and free Gillian, Boots, Grandma, and the rest of Massachusetts. On the other hand, judging from Dad, the only thing princes knew how to do was chase after princesses. Maybe she'd find a different kind of hero.

As Julie got closer, the castle filled the sky. It was a mountain of stone turrets and parapets. Arrow slits scarred the towers, and the gargoyles guarded the battlements. She halted. It looked exactly like an evil castle from a storybook illustration.

Of course it did, she told herself. It *was* the evil castle from storybook illustrations. But that didn't mean she wouldn't find help here.

A shadow crossed over her, and Julie looked up to see an emerald green dragon disappear into one of the castle turrets. A few seconds later, the giant door creaked open, and she saw a half-dozen figures pour onto the drawbridge.

Julie's first impulse was to run back to the beanstalk, but she forced herself to stand still. She *wanted* to meet these people, she reminded herself. "Hello!" she called, and waved. "Help! I need help!"

As they ran across the drawbridge and onto the clouds, Julie saw that they weren't people. Not exactly. She counted three goblins, two trolls, and one woman with a sheep's head. Each of the goblins had an ax strapped to his back, and the trolls and the woman each held a coil of rope. Without pausing, without even glancing at Julie, they barreled past her. "Hey, come back!" she called.

Reaching Julie's beanstalk, the goblins tied the ropes to their waists and then scurried down the stalk. The trolls and the woman encircled the beanstalk and uncoiled the ropes with practiced ease. From below the clouds, Julie heard *smack-thunk-smack*. The beanstalk tip trembled, and then it swayed.

"My beanstalk!" she shouted. "What are you doing?"

"Pull!" a goblin shouted from below.

The ropes went taut, and the trolls and the woman braced themselves and pulled back on the ropes. As the beanstalk tipped and fell through the clouds, the three goblins with their axes were lifted back up to safety.

A deep voice said behind her, "You do not look like Jack."

Julie spun around to face a monster. She shrieked and stumbled backward as he towered over her. The moon was behind him, framing him in its blue-white glow. She couldn't see his eyes; they were sunken in fur. Tusks protruded from the fur around his mouth. His dark velvet cape cloaked his body, but she saw the glint of claws on his massive paws.

A second later, she recognized him. She'd never met him in person before, but there was no question who he was. "You're the Beast," she said out loud. "Beauty's Beast."

He inclined his head. "Once upon a time, I was," he said. "Now I am no one's Beast. Many years ago, I sent Beauty down to the world. As a beast, I would not be welcome in the world below. But Beauty . . . I could not bear to see her live in this place."

He sent her away? Of all the fairy-tale couples she'd heard of, Beauty and the Beast should have lasted. Their love was true. In their fairy tale, they didn't simply kiss and marry; they became friends first. The only other fairy-tale love that came close was Rapunzel and her prince, since they had time together in Rapunzel's tower. For the Beast to send Beauty away . . . Julie looked around. What was so horrible about this place that he'd sent her away? Across the fields of moonlit clouds, Julie saw stalks burst up through the white. She counted nearly a dozen. Elves and goblins leapt onto the backs of winged lizards and flying horses and flew toward the beanstalk tips. Above them, millions of stars filled the sky—more stars than she'd ever seen from her yard at home, more stars than she'd known were in the sky.

"Why have you come here?" the Beast asked. "You did not come from the Wild, and you are not Jack. Who are you? Why are you here?"

"I'm Rapunzel's daughter," Julie said automatically. After a second, she added, "And Rapunzel's prince's daughter too." Even, she thought, if he didn't remember that all the time. "My mother has been kidnapped, and my father"— she paused—"is in danger. Three other people were kidnapped too: Sleeping Beauty, Rumpelstiltskin, and his son. Please, I need your help. *They* need your help."

The Beast was silent. Julie couldn't read his expression. He had to know her mother, she thought. All fairy-tale characters knew Zel. Did Mom know the Beast was here? Did she know he'd sent his Beauty away? It seemed sad, and so unfair.

"I think my mom's being held in Disneyland," Julie said. The dragon had mentioned a castle, and Rumpelstiltskin had said that the original plan was for Dad to kiss Sleeping Beauty in the Disneyland castle. "My dad's trying to save her, but he's walking—flying—right into a trap. If you have a flying carpet or a broomstick or a spare dragon, maybe I can catch him and stop him before it's too late."

"It is already too late," the Beast said.

Julie felt as if her stomach dropped into her shoes. "It can't be too late," she said. Only a few minutes had passed since Dad and the dragon had flown out of the Grand Canyon. It couldn't be too late. She could still catch him.

"Perhaps you do not know how serious things are," he said.

Julie knew it was serious. She'd been swallowed whole by a wolf. She'd nearly been scorched by a dragon.

"Come. I will show you." In a swirl of cape, the Beast strode over the clouds. Mist circled him as he walked. He halted at a gap in the clouds and pointed down to the earth below. Julie looked down.

Below, so far below that her head spun, she saw a street filled with white, gold, and emerald neon. She saw a fountain, a mini-volcano, and a pyramid, plus a red-white-and-blue castle and a replica Eiffel Tower, all so small that they looked like toys. Beyond the neon city center, white and yellow lights spread out along ordinary streets and then faded into the darkness of desert.

"Las Vegas," the Beast said.

But this castle was over Arizona. How could she be looking down at Nevada? They hadn't walked more than a few feet. How could the clouds have drifted so far so fast? "I don't understand," she said. "How are we over a different state?"

"Wherever you are, if you plant a magic bean, it grows into a beanstalk that reaches to the giant's castle in the clouds," the Beast said. "We have discovered that the reverse is also true: from the giant's castle, you can reach anywhere."

Julie gawked at him. Anywhere? Then that meant . . . She could reach Disneyland from here!

"From here, we can see all that we miss in the world below," he said. "It is somewhat ironic. For many long years, this has been our torment. There is so much that we miss. This—watching the world from afar and never being part of it—was not what we imagined our lives would be like when we left the Wild. But now, our torment is our salvation. Our separation from the world has proved to be our best protection."

Her parents were just a few steps away and several miles straight down! This was incredible! Better than incredible!

"Come and look here," the Beast said. "You'll understand once you see." He pointed toward another gap in the clouds, only a few feet away.

Her heart sang. She wasn't too late; she was early! Using the clouds, she could reach Mom before Dad did. She could prevent the last fairy-tale trap. She could save them!

Kneeling on the clouds, she looked where the Beast pointed. Below, she saw darkness. "I don't see anything . . ." she began. Wait, was it moving? The earth below undulated like waves. Maybe it wasn't land; maybe she was over ocean.

"Now look here."

She looked up and saw he'd moved farther east to another gap in the clouds. She followed him and again looked down at writhing blackness.

"And here," he said.

Julie looked down another hole to see the same sight. "I don't understand," she said. "What am I supposed to be seeing?"

Gently, he said, "The Wild."

She swallowed hard and looked again. "Where?" she asked. All she saw was darkness. She couldn't tell where the Wild stopped and the real world began. "Is this Massachusetts?" she asked, but knew as she said it that it was worse than just Massachusetts. His shadowed eyes watched her. "Has it taken New York?" Millions of people lived in New York. If the Wild swallowed New York, that meant millions more fairy-tale events to fuel the Wild.

"New York was lost last night," he said.

"How far?" she whispered. "DC? The whole East Coast?"

"It passed the Mississippi this afternoon. An hour ago, it swallowed Texas and spread into northern Mexico," the Beast said. He led her back to the clouds above Las Vegas. She looked down. Darkness inched across the city. Half of the Las Vegas lights were now gone, swallowed by the darkness, swallowed by the Wild. "In a few hours, the Wild will cover the entire continent. Very soon, this castle will be the only safe place left."

Her knees felt like jelly. She'd never imagined it was this bad.

"So you see, we cannot allow you to leave," he said. His voice was soft—kind, even—and full of pity. "If we allow a beanstalk to stand long enough for you to climb down . . . The Wild is spreading too far and too fast for us to risk it."

"But the Wild isn't in California yet!" Julie said. She could still reach Mom and Dad. She could still—

"I have a responsibility to the creatures who live here," the Beast said. "I cannot allow you to endanger us." He laid a heavy paw on her shoulder. "This is your home now." His other arm swept across the skyscape and the castle.

He was keeping her here? He couldn't! "You have to let me go!" Julie said. She heard her voice squeak like a little kid's and didn't care. "Please, it's not too late!" She tried to dig her heels into the clouds. Mist swirled around her feet.

"Believe me when I say that I am sorry," he said. "This is not a life that I would wish on anyone, to be confined in the clouds." He sighed like a gust of wind. "That is why I sent Beauty away. In retrospect, I should not have done so."

"Please, let me go!" She was so close! Julie felt tears prick her eyes. Dad was the one who was supposed to be walking into a trap, yet *she* was the one caught like a fly in a spider's web.

"You will be safe here," the Beast said. "Perhaps not happy, but safe."

Julie felt her pocket with her elbow. The magic beans were still there. If she could escape the Beast, then she could drop one down a hole in the clouds—maybe a hole directly over Disneyland! It was her only hope. As soon as the Beast was distracted . . . If he was ever distracted . . .

"Or at least as safe as any of us," he amended. "There are some who believe it is hopeless. Right now, inside the castle, Jack's giant is writing and rewriting his story, in hopes of changing his fate in the Wild. But I believe—"

Changing his fate? Julie'd never heard of any fairy-tale character doing such a thing. "Can he do that?" Could the giant really rewrite his fairy tale?

The Beast hesitated. "There is no one to hear his new story. It cannot be a real fairy tale until it is told to people. But the giant believes all other hope is lost. *I* do not! I swear to you that I will fight to defend our home. As long as I have breath in my body, you will be safe here." He raised his voice so that it carried to the creatures across the clouds. "The Wild will not take us!"

Suddenly, a beanstalk punched through the clouds only a few feet away. Another poked through behind her. Elves (tiny, red-clothed elves from the Elves and the Shoemaker story) swarmed around them. One of them pressed something into Julie's hands, and she found herself in a line of elves, holding on to one of the ropes. Other elves swarmed down the beanstalk. On command, she pulled with them as the beanstalk swayed and fell.

"Why are you destroying the beanstalks? Is this your plan to stop the Wild?" she asked the Beast as he grabbed onto a rope near the next beanstalk.

"The Wild can't take the castle if it can't reach it," the Beast said. "Destroying the stalks will keep us safe." A team of bears joined him with more ropes, and a half-dragon woman and a hedgehog boy clambered down and efficiently felled two stalks.

More beanstalks poked though the clouds, and Julie grabbed another rope with the shoemaker's elves. Beanstalks, she realized, were flying up from everywhere the Wild was—and that was most of the country. She understood why the giant thought this was hopeless. She'd never imagined the Wild would spread so far. "It's my fault," Julie said half to herself. "I knew better, and I let Dad walk into trap after trap." Everything that had happened since

Prince's return—maybe even *including* his return—had been a setup. And she hadn't stopped it. She hadn't even seen it. The Wild had been safe and secure under Julie's bed. It could have stayed there indefinitely if she hadn't let the third blind mouse run in. Or if she hadn't let Dad pick up the glass slipper in Times Square. Or kill the wolf. Or fight the dragon.

"It's not your fault, child," the Beast said. "It's mine."

His fault? What did he mean? She tore her eyes from the beanstalk to look at him. Moonlight reflected off his velvet cape, but his thick fur seemed to absorb all light. It was like looking at a living shadow.

"I should never have sent Beauty away," he said.

His Beauty was undoubtedly trapped in the Wild by now, just like Boots and Gillian and Grandma and everyone else. But that wasn't his fault. He shouldn't blame himself. "You didn't know this would happen," she said. Julie should have known where Dad's actions would lead. She should have fought harder to make Dad turn around and go home. She should have stopped Dad from flying out of Jack's apartment. She should have guessed it was all a trap. Stupid, stupid, stupid, she thought.

He shook his head. "I should have foreseen this."

Before she could reply, tiny voices shouted, "It's away!" The rope jerked forward. Julie and the elves leaned backward and pulled. Yet another beanstalk burst through the clouds. After a delay, a trio of flying monkeys swarmed down it.

Behind her, she heard a thundering crash. Everyone froze and all eyes turned toward the castle. Julie saw a green beanstalk shoot up through one of the castle turrets. Stones tumbled down, crashing into the walls and smashing down on the drawbridge.

"To the castle!" the Beast shouted. With a cry, a half dozen fairies flew toward the wrecked turret. Two griffins circled and then dove.

A bird-woman soared over them. "Stalks to the north!" she cried.

Across the skyscape, Julie saw more beanstalks stab through the clouds. Mist puffed around them. Pixies swarmed over the clouds to perch on the tips, lighting them like beacons for the creatures with axes to see. The creatures spread out and scurried down stalks.

"There have never been so many!" the Beast said.

"The Wild must have noticed that you were chopping down the beanstalks," Julie said. The Beast and his friends were chopping them all down before anyone could climb up a stalk, meet the giant, and complete the Jack and the Beanstalk story. The Wild must have realized that no one was completing the story! Now that it had noticed, it was sending up as many beanstalks as it could. This was a deliberate attack. It was sheer awful coincidence that the attack had started just as Julie arrived.

Or was it? The Wild couldn't be attacking *because* Julie had arrived, could it? No, that was ridiculous. Why would the Wild care about her? Granted, she was the one who had stopped it last time . . . She pushed the thought out of her mind and concentrated on pulling up the rope. She was sweating now, and her hair stuck to her forehead as if it was glued in place.

All around them, beanstalks sprang through the clouds, one after another after another shooting up in plumes of mist. Julie looked out over the clouds and saw a sea of green tips, as if the clouds were a moonlit field. There were hundreds. Thousands. Pixies flitted over them, vastly outnumbered.

"Oh, wow," she whispered as her heart sank. There were so many. Too many.

"Fire!" the Beast yelled. "We need fire!" At his command, winged creatures flew over the beanstalk tips while elves, mounted on their backs, lit the beanstalks on fire with torches. A seven-headed dragon shot flame from each of its heads. Across the clouds, beanstalks burned. Inky smoke stained the night sky. But still, more beanstalks burst through the clouds. There were now hundreds of thousands of leafy green stalks.

They'd never be able to stop them all. They were going to lose the castle! "You have to let me find my parents!" Julie called after him. "They can help! I can bring them here to help!"

CRASH! A green stalk suddenly burst through the drawbridge. Splinters of wood shot into the air. Another stalk crashed through the battlements. Stones rained down on the clouds. Julie heard screams. Handing his rope to an ogre, the Beast charged toward the castle.

Looking around, Julie knew she had one choice. She *had* to stop this. She had to find her parents, stop the kidnappers, and stop the Wild. And she wasn't going to be able to do any of those things if she stayed here and fought a losing battle. Getting to her feet, she raced toward the castle.

Up ahead, she spotted a hole in the clouds. Dropping to her knees, Julie looked down through the puffs of gray. She saw the twinkle of thousands of lights curling and stretching in every direction and then ending to the east in darkness. Was that desert? Or ocean? If it was the Pacific Ocean . . . She jumped to her feet and ran to the next hole. Same thing: a twinkle of lights that ended in a stretch of black. She had to have found the ocean! All she needed to do was follow the edge south until she saw Disneyland.

South, south, south . . . As she ran, she reached into her pocket and pulled out the bottle of magic beans. She knelt by another gap in the clouds. No Disney. She ran to the next. Not yet. Another. No. And another.

Finally, Julie found it. Kneeling beside the hole in the clouds, she stared down at the gleaming lights of Disneyland, which made it easily recognizable from the clouds. She saw the shapes of the rides—the white peaks of Space Mountain, the tent-like roofs of carousels, a man-made circular river . . .

She dropped the bean.

"Come on," she whispered. "Grow! Grow!"

Nothing.

Still nothing.

Wait, was that . . . Yes, there! From above, the stalk looked like a mass of leaves shooting upward with the power of a rocket. She scrambled back just as the beanstalk burst through the clouds. The tip curled in front of Julie's nose. She glanced back one more time at the sea of burning beanstalks and at the shattered castle.

Vines crawled like black snakes across the face of the stone. They were losing—the Wild was coming. Feeling sick, Julie jumped on the stalk and began to climb down.

## Chapter Fourteen
### *Down the Beanstalk*

Cool air circled Julie as she climbed down through the clouds. Faster, she urged herself. Faster! If the Beast and his creatures spotted her beanstalk, they'd chop it down, and she'd fall. She had to reach the bottom before that happened. She lowered herself down to the next leaf stem and then the next.

As she climbed lower, the shouts and cries from the fairy-tale creatures faded, carried away by the wind. Soon, there was silence. She heard only the wordless wind and the rustle of the leaves. Had she climbed too low to hear the battle above, or was it over? Had the Wild won? She wasn't about to climb back up and check. She continued down.

How long would the Beast and his creatures be able to fight? They might last for a while, but could they stop hundreds of thousands beanstalks? Or millions? Sooner or later, they would lose and the last safe place would fall.

As the leaves rustled around her, she caught glimpses of the Los Angeles lights below. Tiny specks, they looked like earthbound stars. She wondered if her mom was down below looking up toward her. Even though Mom didn't have to hide away like the Beast, she *did* have to keep her existence a secret too. Julie thought of Dad's reaction when Mom had told him he needed to hide who he was. *You fought for freedom,* he had said. *How is it freedom to hide who you are?* Maybe Mom wasn't so different from the Beast after all. She was hiding in plain sight, but she was still hiding. She was pretending to be ordinary and trying to blend in. Julie did the same thing at school, pretending that she fit in—hiding who she was, what she'd done, and where she'd come from. That wasn't right either.

At least the Beast didn't have to lie about his name or his past. He didn't have to lie to people who loved him, like Rumpelstiltskin felt he had to do. Rumpelstiltskin had kept who he was a secret from his own son. Was that so much better than the Beast physically hiding himself up in the clouds? All the hiding, all the secrecy, all the fear . . . it wasn't fair to any of them.

She thought about Henry, finding out for the first time that his father was a fairy-tale character one moment and then being carried away by a dragon the next. He was, she thought, having a *much* worse day than she was.

Poor Henry. Maybe her parents would help save him after Julie rescued them. Maybe they could all escape somewhere together . . .

But how exactly was she going to rescue her parents? She had no allies, no magic, no plan, and the Wild was growing larger and stronger every minute. Even if she did rescue them, how were they going to escape the Wild, especially if the last safe place was gone? Was this a doomed quest?

Just take it one step at a time, she told herself. Or one leaf at a time. Her arms were starting to ache, and her palms were developing blisters. The skin of the beanstalk was as rough as sandpaper. She began to wonder, had Dad planned to return to the Grand Canyon for her after he saved Mom? Or was leaving her just a choice he made out of necessity, like when she had left him behind in the Wild? She'd had a choice: stay with Dad inside the Wild or walk through a motel room door in his castle to the wishing well. It hadn't been an easy decision. Had it been as hard for Dad?

Julie heard a faint rumble, but this time it was coming from below. She looked down, but all she could see was the dense green of beanstalk leaves. Climbing lower, she heard the sound of glass shattering. People were yelling, their voices blurring together into one angry scream. What was happening on the ground? She'd expected, well, Disneyland below her. Happiest place on earth. This sounded anything but happy.

The beanstalk trembled, and Julie clung to the stalk. *That* didn't feel like wind. Her heart thudded faster. How far was she from the bottom? "Don't fall," she whispered to the stalk. The beanstalk lurched and swayed. Julie squeezed her eyes shut and hugged it. When the beanstalk steadied, she began clambering down as fast as she could, chanting to herself, "Don't fall, don't fall, don't fall."

She heard a shout from below: "Someone's climbing down the beanstalk!"

Oh, no. She froze. What should she do?

"Cut it down! Find an ax! Find a chainsaw!"

No, no, no! Julie looked up. She'd never make it back to the clouds before they (whoever "they" were) found a way to chop the stalk down. And besides, she couldn't go back there. The Wild was there. "Don't!" she shouted. "Don't chop it down!"

"Someone *is* there!" she heard.

She had to convince them she wasn't an enemy. She had an idea. "Help!" she cried. "Please, help! I'm in the beanstalk! Please, help me down!"

"Someone's trapped up there!" she heard. "It sounds like a kid!"

Yes! "Please, help!" she called. In another burst of inspiration, Julie added, "I want my mommy!" That wasn't even a lie. The beanstalk stopped shaking, and she scrambled down the remaining leaves.

Hands reached up to pull her off the stalk. She began making sobbing noises. "Oh, thank you, thank you, thank you! It was horrible!" Once she started to fake-cry, she nearly started to cry for real. Comforting hands patted her. She wished she could tell them the truth. It *was* horrible. She doubted these strangers even knew how horrible. Spreading her hands, she peeked up at the people around her. She was enclosed in a ring of very agitated men and women.

"Where are your parents?" someone asked her.

A real tear escaped down her cheek. Where were they? She knew the answer to that. Could she say the real answer? "I think . . . the castle." She wished these people were really her rescuers.

"Oh, you poor dear," a woman said.

Her heart thudded faster. Poor dear? Why? "What's wrong with the castle?"

The woman wrapped her arm around Julie's shoulders. "Better if you don't look," she said. "It will be destroyed soon enough. We're wiping this place clean of all fairy tales." She beckoned to a police officer, standing next to a streetlamp. "This little girl shouldn't be here. Can you take her somewhere safe?"

No! She couldn't—

The crowd cheered as the beanstalk creaked and swayed. "Bring it down!" people shouted. "Destroy the fairy tales!" Both the policeman and the woman looked up, momentarily distracted from Julie. Seizing the opportunity, she shook off the woman's arm. She ran under shimmering lights and past a row of pink and purple boats and then splashed down into ankle-deep water. Wading through an archway, Julie climbed out of the water and hid behind the arch. Had anyone seen her? Was anyone chasing her? Heart pounding, she peered out.

People were pointing upward and shouting. Julie heard a loud snap and then a whoosh of wind. A few seconds later . . . *crash!* She clutched the walls as everything shook.

Outside, the crowd cheered. Julie shrank back. They'd done it, she realized. They'd knocked down the beanstalk. She began to shake. She was nearly on that beanstalk when it fell. If she'd climbed any slower . . . If they hadn't believed she was an ordinary girl . . . Huddling in the archway, she wished she could stay here and hide—though she wondered where exactly "here" was. For the first time, Julie glanced around her. Dolls had been yanked from their pedestals and tossed around the room. Plastic arms and legs littered the AstroTurf floor. Perky suns and clouds had been torn from the walls. From another part of the ride, she heard distorted tinny music: " . . . *a world of laughter, a world of joy* . . ." She stared at the wreckage.

The crowd had trashed It's a Small World.

It didn't make sense. Small World? Why wreck Small

World? She thought of what the woman had said: they were here to wipe the place clean of fairy tales. They're scared, she answered herself. The Wild has eaten half the country, and they're scared. So they came to a place full of fairy tales and set about destroying it, as if that would help.

And Mom and Dad were out there in the heart of it.

Taking a deep breath, Julie hopped again into the ankle-deep water and waded past the pink and purple boats. Climbing onto the shore, she looked out between bushes shaped like elephants and dancing hippos. She saw people. Lots and lots of very angry, very loud people. Dense crowds clogged the sidewalks, lawns, and rides. She couldn't see beyond them. I'll never be able to sneak by, she thought.

Wait—she didn't have to sneak! She wasn't a fairy-tale character. She looked perfectly ordinary. What if she pretended she was one of them? That shouldn't be too hard, she thought. She'd been pretending she was one of them her whole life.

Spotting a pack of teenagers, Julie hopped out of the water and ran toward them. "This way!" she shouted. She pointed toward the center of the park. The kids roared and changed direction. She trailed behind as they shoved through the crowd. Before they could notice she wasn't one of them, Julie ducked into a ride and hopped inside a giant pale purple teacup.

Wow, she hadn't thought that would actually work.

Grinning, Julie peeked up over the rim of the teacup. Her grin faded. Beyond the teacups, it was bad. Lit by the lights of the rides, Crayola-bright debris covered the street. Wreckage blocked the opening to Peter Pan's Flight. The caterpillar from the Alice in Wonderland ride had been smashed, and the oversized flowers had been crushed and trampled. Horses from a carousel lay on their sides like wounded animals. Flags and signs hung limp and torn from lampposts. Cars from Mr. Toad's Wild Ride had been tossed across the serpentine to lie upside down in a heap.

Above it all loomed Sleeping Beauty's castle.

The castle was encased in thorns.

Roses chased up the turrets. Thick knots of branches with thorns as long as Julie's arm squeezed around it. She could barely see the tips of the flags at the top of the castle. And, high above them, she saw the silhouette of a figure on a broomstick, circling the top of the tower, illuminated by the dozens of floodlights aimed at the castle.

Dad!

No, it wasn't Dad. As the figure circled closer, Julie saw white frizzed hair and a billowing cloak. On the back of the broomstick, she saw the silhouette of a cat.

"Grandma," she breathed. "Boots!"

Grandma and Boots were here! They'd evaded the Wild! But how? Why were they here, nearly three thousand miles from home? Had they come to rescue Mom? Had they seen

Dad? Julie wanted to shout out to them. But they'd never hear her over the roar of the crowd, and the people who would hear her . . . Julie did *not* want to draw their attention. She needed to pretend she was one of them. She was stuck on her own. For now.

Just knowing that Grandma and Boots were out there, though, made her feel like she'd eaten five chocolate bars and was full of sugar energy. She took quick stock: Sleeping Beauty was clearly here, which meant that the dragon was too, probably with Henry, Rumpelstiltskin, and maybe Mom! Dad couldn't be far behind.

He'd enter from the front, she thought. That was how a fairy-tale prince would do it: storm the castle from the front gate. She crawled out of the teacup and plunged back out into the crowd.

Zigzagging through the mob, Julie crossed over a bridge and then ducked down behind battered shrubbery, sculpted into the shape of Pinocchio and a donkey (both now headless).

For a minute, Julie simply crouched there, panting. And then she gathered her courage and looked out. From here, she could see a stage in front of the castle. It had been abandoned mid-performance. Costumes and props and equipment were strewn all over. A single microphone stood on a podium, spotlight still fixed on it, as if waiting for someone to step forward and yell, "Stop!" But no one did.

Beneath the floodlights, the plaza in front of the stage was nearly as bright as day. A TV crew was filming the wreckage of Main Street, and Julie saw people dart in and out of shops. A constant hum of sometimes distant and sometimes scarily close shouting filled the air. Was it like this everywhere, she wondered, or just Disneyland? Looking up, Julie saw that Grandma and Boots still circled the castle, silhouetted against the night sky. There was no sign of Dad. Maybe he was already here. Maybe he was inside . . .

Suddenly, like a sunrise staining the sky, all the brambles around the castle blossomed into red roses and green leaves. Staring, Julie forgot to breathe. Oh, wow, what could this mean? Seconds later, the roses and leaves withered and dropped, and the thorns curled back in on themselves, receding down the stone walls of the castle.

Dad had done it!

Julie didn't know whether to cheer or cry. He'd completed his quest and sprung the final trap. He'd awakened Sleeping Beauty.

Shouts echoed throughout the park, and people poured toward the castle. From Tomorrowland, a pack of policemen charged onto the plaza. From Adventureland, a TV crew raced over a bridge. Now that the thorns were gone, Julie could see that all the stained glass windows of the castle had been reduced to broken shards. Someone had scrawled *Once Upon a Never* and *Happily Never After* amid various curse words in bright red over the castle facade. Inside the archway to Fantasyland, the mosaic of Sleeping Beauty was shattered. Tiles lay scattered on the ground.

Then the castle door flung open. Two figures tumbled out, one with bright yellow hair and the other—Dad! Beside him, Sleeping Beauty (a very awake Sleeping Beauty) pointed and shouted at the growing, growling crowd.

Police swarmed forward.

Oh, no, she had to do something! Julie hadn't come this far for Dad to be arrested now! Julie leapt up.

Sparkles twinkled in the castle archway, and the fairy godmother Bobbi suddenly appeared inside the shimmering glitter. She looked like the quintessential fairy godmother: iridescent butterfly wings, a pink gown, a sparkling wand. The police fell back, and there was an instant of silence as the entire crowd gasped in unison.

Bobbi laughed, and the sound echoed across the park. "Oh, you can't have him yet. We aren't finished with him. He has one more story to complete." She waved her wand at Dad, and the prince vanished in a swirl of sparkles.

"No!" Julie yelled.

With a flick of her wrist, Bobbi vanished. Reappearing on the opposite side of the archway, she knelt and held out her hands to catch a fat green frog mid-leap. A frog! She'd turned Dad into a frog!

Fluttering her wings, the fairy godmother rose into the air as the nearest policeman lunged for her. Where was Grandma? Why didn't she do something? Julie looked up at the empty sky as a second policeman raised his gun and aimed at Bobbi.

Bobbi and the frog/Dad vanished.

*Crack.*

"Dad!" Julie cried. Her scream was drowned out by the screams of the crowd.

## Chapter Fifteen
### *Disneyland*

Julie crouched behind the battered bushes as the mob panicked. Some ran away from the castle, trampling across the bridges and sidewalks. Some rushed toward it. Fights broke out. Julie hugged her arms, instinctively making herself as small as possible.

What should she do? What *could* she do? Dad was captured (and a frog). Mom was captured. Henry and Rumpelstiltskin, captured. Sleeping Beauty . . . Julie peeked out again. Sleeping Beauty was being arrested, and two men were bashing at the castle door with a pole from a carousel horse. Grandma and Boots were nowhere to be seen.

I failed, Julie thought. We lost. We lost thoroughly and completely. The kidnappers won. Soon, the Wild would cover the entire continent and begin to spread to the rest of the world. Julie felt her eyes fill up with tears. She'd failed, failed, failed. Everyone was going to be trapped inside fairy tales. She was never going to see her family again. And there was nothing she could do about it.

The only way to stop the Wild was with a wish in the wishing well, but the well was thousands of miles from here. Last time, she had found a magic door in a castle that had led to the Wishing Well Motel. She couldn't count on that happening again.

Her breath caught in her throat. Wait. Just wait. What if she could *make* it happen? What if she turned her experience into a fairy tale? By its own rules, the Wild reenacted fairy tales. If her story was a real fairy tale, then the Wild would *have* to include a motel room door inside its castles, just like it had to put an oven in its gingerbread houses.

Could she do it? She remembered how the Beast had told her about the giant writing stories to try to change his fate. The Beast had said the giant would fail because he hadn't told his stories to anyone. But here at Disneyland, there were thousands of people to tell. If she told her story to everyone, maybe it would become a real fairy tale!

It was a crazy thought. It meant revealing her family secret in the most public way possible. But did she have any better ideas?

Julie peered out through the bushes at the castle. As she'd noticed before, the stage in front of the castle looked as if it had been abandoned mid-performance—amid the wreckage of costumes and props, a microphone still stood on a podium. If she told her story here in front of all these people . . . She had to at least try!

Gathering her courage, Julie crept out from behind the

bushes and joined the mob. Immediately, the flood of men and women swept her forward. She was tossed back and forth as she zigzagged toward the stage, and as soon as a path cleared for an instant, she ran up the stairs to the stage and climbed onto the podium.

This will never work, she thought. There's no way that the microphone is still on. She tapped it. See, nothing. Examining it, she flipped a switch and tapped it again.

Speakers thumped across the park.

Whoa.

Okay, this was it. She hoped this wasn't a stupid idea. All her life, she'd been trained to hide who she was . . . She hoped Mom understood. "Um . . . Hello? Everyone, listen to me," she said into the microphone. "Everything you're doing here isn't helping. You can't stop the Wild this way." Her words echoed back through the speakers, but they had no effect on the crowd. People continued to shove and shout on the plaza in front of her. "Listen to me! I think I know how to stop it!"

Sparkles fluttered around her.

Julie felt her stomach sink. Oh, no.

From the top of the podium stairs, the fairy godmother waved at her. She wasn't, Julie noticed immediately, holding the frog. What had she done with Dad? Bobbi shook her finger in a tsking motion. "My dear, you're not ruining this for me. I have the chance to be great again, and no little brat is going to take that from me," she said merrily. The mike picked up her words and amplified them across the park. She raised her wand and pointed it at Julie.

Julie shrank back. The lip of the podium was behind her. It was a twenty-foot drop to the pavement below. Trapped, trapped, trapped! "Don't!" she cried, throwing her arms up over her face.

Wind rushed against her, and Julie heard Bobbi say, "You!"

Julie lowered her arms to see Grandma, mounted on her broomstick, between her and Bobbi. Perched in mid-air, Boots hissed at Bobbi.

"Don't you point that stick at my granddaughter," Grandma snarled. She pointed her finger at Bobbi, and a shot of black dust flew from her fingertips. Bobbi vanished and reappeared a few feet to the left. She aimed her wand at Grandma.

"Watch out!" Julie shouted.

Boots leapt off the back of the broomstick onto the podium as Grandma dodged. A bolt of sparkles slammed into a lamppost, and it collapsed in a poof of smoke. In its place sat a pumpkin. Grandma zapped back. Bobbi ducked, and a shower of snakes fell from a castle flag and plummeted into the moat.

"Get down," Boots said in a voice low enough for only Julie to hear.

She dropped to her knees beside her brother. Whipping her wand in a circle, the fairy godmother shot a cyclone of sparkles at Gothel. Julie flattened onto her stomach and covered her head. Missing Grandma by inches, the sparkles bored a hole into the wall of the castle.

Hands raised, black lightning shooting from her fingertips, Grandma flew on her broomstick at Bobbi. Bobbi soared upward, wings flapping, and Grandma chased her.

Julie didn't move. She'd nearly been . . . If Grandma hadn't come . . .

Boots wound around Julie. "Unless you're planning to burst into song, which I don't advise, we should get off this stage," he said under his breath so the microphone wouldn't hear him.

Julie got to her feet. She couldn't leave. The fact that Bobbi had tried to stop her . . . That meant she was on the right track. It meant that she had been right. She *could* affect the Wild! She had to at least try. Her hands shook. She wrapped them around the stalk of the microphone.

"Um, Julie?" Boots said. "Hostile mob? Remember? We should exit, stage left."

"You have to listen to me!" she shouted into the mike. At that moment, above the castle, Grandma shot a shower of sparks into the night sky. Stunned by the sight, the mob fell silent for an instant. An instant was all Julie needed.

She plunged into the silence: "I can tell you how to stop the Wild!"

Now *that* caught the crowd's attention.

She took a deep breath. "I stopped the Wild six weeks ago. My mother and father stopped it five hundred years ago. My name is Julie. I'm Rapunzel's daughter." There. She'd said it. Her secret was out. And the crowd was listening.

Still under his breath, Boots said, "Zel is *so* going to kill you."

Julie ignored him and kept talking. She told them how the Wild had escaped from under her bed, how she'd gone into the fairy-tale woods to rescue her mom, how instead she'd found her dad inside a castle with a magic door—a motel room door. She told them how she'd chosen to walk through the door to the wishing well at the Wishing Well Motel, even though it meant leaving her dad behind. Lastly, she told them about the wish she'd made that had returned the world to normal and had transformed the Wild back to a tangle of vines under her bed.

She finished, and the mob was silent. At least three news cameras swept the crowd, clearly taping, recording and broadcasting everything she'd just said.

Julie leaned into the microphone again. "This is how we defeat the Wild: we *change* it. Tell this story to each other. Tell it to everyone you meet. If it's told often enough, then the Wild will be forced to include a door to the well in all of its castles. And then someone can walk through the door and wish this all away!"

Had she reached them? Did they believe her? Would they retell the story to each other? She hoped so. She had nothing else to say, and her secret was out. Either this would work or it wouldn't. She'd done the best she could. She switched off the microphone.

The crowd began to murmur.

Above Space Mountain in Tomorrowland, Julie saw sparks fly like out-of-control fireworks, lighting up the night. Was Grandma winning or losing? She couldn't tell, and there wasn't anything that Julie could do to help her. "Come on," Julie said to Boots. "Let's go save Mom." Taking a deep breath, she climbed down from the podium and walked across the stage toward the castle.

People stared, and then they parted for her. With Boots trotting beside her, Julie walked into the archway, past the police who held Sleeping Beauty, and up to the castle door. Now what? She had to get inside. She felt her back itch as she tried not to think about the thousands of people staring at her.

Boots rose up onto his hind legs. "Excuse me," he said to the two men who had been trying to knock down the castle door. "Yes, you. Can you please open that for us? Rapunzel is inside, and we'd like to rescue her."

The nearest man opened and closed his mouth twice.

"What?" Boots said. "I said 'please.' Oh, and can I have your hat? I'm feeling a little naked here, people."

A policeman plucked the hat off the man's head and tossed it to Boots. The cat swept him a bow and then placed the hat on his head over his ears. He gestured toward the door, and Julie stepped back.

The mob was silent as the men bashed down the castle door.

"That was brave," Julie said to Boots. The mob could have panicked at the sight of a talking cat.

"I assume you have a plan for once we get inside?" he whispered.

"Not really, no," she said.

Boots sighed. "I hate being your sidekick."

Despite everything, Julie smiled. "Good to see you too."

With a loud crack, the wood around the doorknob splintered. Leaning their shoulders against it, the men shoved it open. One of them started to step through into the castle, but the other grabbed his arm. "You don't know what's in there. There could be more of them." He nodded over at Boots.

Boots fluffed his tail and trotted toward the door. "Uh, thanks," Julie said as she passed by them.

"Julie!" a voice called from the other side of the archway. She turned her head and saw Rose—Sleeping Beauty—still held by police. Her hair was disheveled, and her eyes were wild. "Watch out for spinning wheels! And swans!"

Spinning wheels? Swans? Poor Rose. Look what her fairy tale had done to her. She wasn't even making sense. Please, Julie thought, let my plan work! "I'll stop the Wild," Julie called to her. "I promise!" She waved to her, the police, and the crowd as she and Boots stepped inside the Disneyland castle.

## Chapter Sixteen
### *Sleeping Beauty's Castle*

Once inside, Julie came face-to-face with six-foot-tall presents with oversized ribbons on top, human-sized snow globes, and an apple as large as a beach ball. Mickey Mouse, Donald Duck, and Goofy heads sat on shelves. "It's like the inside of a giant toy box," she whispered to Boots.

Trays of eye shadow, tubes of lipstick, canisters of hair spray, and dozens of combs were strewn across a counter. Glittering costumes hung from rows of racks. Fluorescent bulbs reflected in the mirrors. This must be a dressing room for the people who dressed up as Disney characters every day. She had expected something more, well, castle-like than costumes and makeup. She'd also been hoping for some sort of sign to where Mom and Dad were. Something like: "Dungeon This Way" or "Prisoners Here!"

Boots trotted across the room to a row of closet doors and sniffed at the bottom of the first one. At the third door, he halted. "Here!"

"You smell them?" Julie hurried across the room.

"Do I look like a bloodhound?" he said. "I heard a frog ribbet."

Dad! "Dad, Mom, we're coming!" She rattled the door handle. Locked! Julie looked around for something heavy to bash against the door, like a fire extinguisher or a mallet or . . . a spinning wheel?

Julie froze. In a dimly lit corner of the room, half obscured by costume racks, a woman sat at a spinning wheel. The wheel clicked as she pushed the foot pedal, and the wheel began to spin.

Uh-oh, Julie thought.

"*Ribbet!*" she heard through the door. Quickly, Julie grabbed the nearest chair and threw it against the door. "Boots, help!" She pounded the door again.

"How?" he asked. "Cats aren't exactly known for their kung fu skills."

When the wheel was whirring full speed, the woman stood up and stepped forward into the greenish fluorescent light. Seeing her face, Julie stopped and stared. The chair slipped out of her hands and clattered to the floor. "Linda?" she said. Linda the librarian? Shouldn't she be in Northboro? Shouldn't she be in the Wild? What was she doing in California inside Sleeping Beauty's castle at a spinning wheel? "What are you doing here?"

"I am fixing what your mother broke," Linda said. "I'm

fixing the stories." She smiled at Julie, her eyes shining. "Soon, everything will be as it should be."

On the other side of the door, Julie heard frantic rib-beting and a soft *splat* sound—it sounded as if her dad was hurling his frog body against the door. She took a step backward. Dad wouldn't be doing that if Linda was here to help. Julie had a very bad feeling about this.

"I had thought it would be enough for the Wild to re-turn temporarily, but it wasn't," Linda said. "All the new stories didn't change the world enough."

"Uh, Julie," Boots said. "I think she's evil."

"Yeah, I think so too," Julie said. Rumpelstiltskin had said that Bobbi had a boss. He'd said there was someone worse. Julie just hadn't expected it to be someone she knew. Linda still looked like the perky, friendly children's librar-ian that Julie had grown up knowing. She had plain brown hair and an ordinary round face with chipmunk cheeks. She wore a preppy brown sweater set and charcoal gray pants. What kind of villain wore a sweater set?

Linda looked offended. "I'm not evil."

"You're trying to take over the world," Julie pointed out. "That's classic evil behavior." She tried to sound brave, but her voice shook, betraying her.

Linda laughed. "I'm not taking over the world," she said. "I'm restoring it. I'm bringing back magic and wonder and justice and adventure and true love."

"Evil *and* insane," Boots hissed, backing up. "Always a charming combination."

Linda frowned at Boots. "I know my actions may seem a little drastic . . ."

"A little?" Boots said sarcastically. "If by 'little,' you mean King Kong caliber."

" . . . but we were never meant to live out of the Wild. We—your mother, your father, the fairy godmother, me— are all pieces of the Wild."

Mom was *not* a piece of the Wild. She was herself. She was more than the fairy-tale Rapunzel. Even Dad had changed in the brief time he'd been here, though he hadn't stopped chasing princesses. "That's not true—" Julie began to object.

"Why else would the Wild shrink when we leave it? We're part of it. We are meant to be in our stories," Linda said. She looked so earnest that Julie shivered. Linda really believed what she was saying. "I tried to live in the world. I truly did. I even tried a wish in the well. But a temporary return of the Wild wasn't enough. The Wild told me it wouldn't be enough, and it was right."

Linda had talked to the Wild? When? How? So far as Julie knew, she was the only one who had ever spoken directly to the Wild, when it had possessed her brother, Boots, and tried to talk her out of saving her mother. "You spoke to it?"

Linda ignored the question. "I want you to understand that this wasn't my first choice," she said, "and I know it's not what you would prefer." Not what she'd *prefer*? The world was being destroyed! All across the continent, people were losing their identities, losing themselves, losing their lives! She'd just seen what a fairy tale had done to Sleeping Beauty. Now—because of Linda—that was happening to millions of people! "But this is the only way," Linda said.

Julie opened her mouth to object. It was not at all the only way. It was the worst—

Looking beyond Julie and Boots, Linda nodded.

"Uh-oh," Boots said. "That's a signal." He spun around and yelped as two oversized swans waddled out from between the costume racks. Swans? For an instant, Julie could only stare. Linda's henchmen were *swans*? Sleeping Beauty had warned her, but . . . swans? Of course, these birds weren't ordinary. For one thing, they were taller than Julie. For another, they wore crowns. They're the swan-men, Julie realized—fairy-tale princes who had been transformed into swans while they were in the Wild. And they were also Boots's worst nightmare.

His fur fluffing out, Boots began to quiver and shake. "Giant birds! Nooo!" Fanning their wings, the swans hissed at Boots.

"Boots!" Julie cried, diving for him. One of the swans

reached out his neck and snapped his beak at her arm. He pinched skin. "Ow!"

Spitting and hissing, Boots lashed his tail and drew his claws.

"Don't you hurt my brother," Julie said, grabbing the chair again. She hefted it up, ready to swing. She'd kick some swan butt if she had to.

"If the cat doesn't meddle, he won't be hurt," Linda said. She sounded impatient, as if she thought they were being a bit silly. The mild tone made her words sound even more frightening. "Guard him, please," she said to the swans.

The two swan-princes flanked the cat like sentries. How many fairy-tale characters did Linda have working for her? How many wanted the Wild to return? Julie'd had no idea that so many were this unhappy with the real world.

"There's no need for unpleasantness," Linda said. "Once the Wild is here, he'll be back in his story, and we won't have a problem. We'll all be friends."

"You won't be friends," Boots said to the swans. "You'll be dinner." He bared his teeth. "Swan à la king."

One of the swans snapped his beak at Boots, inches from his tail. Julie stepped closer with the chair raised over her head.

"Julie, put the chair down," Linda said.

She didn't. "You have what you want," Julie said. "The Wild's coming. You won. Please, let my family go." She didn't want to face the Wild alone. What if her story didn't work? What if the door to the well didn't appear? At least they could be together when the Wild came. At least she could say goodbye before she forgot them forever.

"I will," Linda said. "There's no more need to keep them. Your father has performed as many fairy-tale moments as I could have wished for, and the Wild is now much too strong for your mother to stop."

Julie lowered the chair. "You will?" Linda was going to let them go? Just like that?

"But *you*, my dear," Linda said. Before Julie could react, Linda lifted the chair out of Julie's hands. "I'm sorry, Julie, but you are a different story. No pun intended." She smiled faintly and set the chair down out of reach. Julie backed away, reaching for something else to defend herself with. A swan-man snapped his beak at her again, stopping her. "As lovely as the tale you told was, the Wild and I have another story in mind for you."

Another story? Julie's eyes flickered to the spinning wheel. Slower now, the wheel still whirred, and the spindle turned. The tip of it, she noticed, was bright silver and very sharp.

"You'll sleep for a hundred years in this very appropriate castle," Linda said, "and then you'll wake to your prince's kiss in the final moment of the Sleeping Beauty story." She grabbed Julie's wrists.

"Hey!" Julie struggled. "Let go of me!"

The frog, her father, started ribbeting frantically behind door number three.

Linda pulled her toward the spinning wheel. Oh, no, no, no, Julie thought. Linda continued in a calm and reasonable voice, "And then, of course, you will forget that you were ever once a girl who walked through a door to a wishing well. It won't matter if there's a door to the well in every castle. You won't know to walk through it. You won't know what wish to make." Julie dug her heels into the carpet. Linda, a foot taller and significantly stronger, dragged her across the floor with ease. "You'll be Sleeping Beauty forevermore. Won't that be nice? You'll be a princess."

"I don't want to be Sleeping Beauty!" Julie twisted her wrists and tried to yank away. "Even Sleeping Beauty doesn't want to be Sleeping Beauty!" It was, as Dad had said, one of the worst fates in the fairy-tale world. Sleeping Beauty was, in essence, denied a fate. She was forced to miss life. There was no hope for escape in the Sleeping Beauty tale. She was exiled from her family, she slept for a hundred years, and then she woke. That was it. The end. If Julie were caught in her tale, she would never have the chance to break free. "Please, not Sleeping Beauty!"

Boots howled. The swans spread their wings around him, and he scratched and bit, defending himself. Imitating him, Julie kicked and scratched and hit Linda.

"Shh, now," Linda said. "It will only hurt for a moment and then you'll be happily-ever-after. Really, this is better for everyone." Julie yanked at Linda's hair. She bit Linda's arm. Linda simply tightened her grip and continued to drag her across the room. The spinning wheel was now only a yard away.

Think, Julie, she told herself. Think! "Please, don't!" Julie begged. "Why are you doing this? I don't believe it's just because you like stories!"

"It's because I like *my* story," Linda said simply. "Your mother took it from me, and I lost my happily-ever-after. I want it back. I want him back."

She had a story? She was a fairy-tale character? "You're from the Wild?" Who was she? She had to be a villain. An evil stepmother, a wicked queen, an angry fairy . . . "Let go of me!" she said, continuing to struggle.

Linda clamped her hand around Julie's wrist hard enough to bruise the skin. She stretched Julie's arm toward the spinning wheel. She was one foot from the spindle now. "I'm sorry," Linda said in a frighteningly calm voice, "but I am not like your mother. I cannot live without my true love. I have to return to him, no matter what the cost."

Him? Him who? Return to him . . . She mentioned a happily-ever-after . . . She's not a villain, Julie realized. She had a happily-ever-after. She's a heroine. Like Mom. Like

Cindy. Like Snow . . . She's a heroine who was separated from her love.

Instantly, Julie knew. *It's my fault,* the Beast had said. *I should never have sent Beauty away.* Linda was Beauty. And Beauty wanted her Beast back.

As Julie struggled, Linda pulled her hand closer and closer to the silver tip of the spindle. One inch from the spindle. "It won't work!" Julie shouted. "When you enter the Wild, the Beast won't be there!"

Linda stopped. "What?"

"You're Beauty," Julie said. "Aren't you?" She had to be right. She had to be! "I met the Beast in the giant's castle in the clouds. He's fighting the Wild. When you go into your fairy tale, he won't be there."

All the blood ran out of Linda's face. She began to tremble. Julie yanked her hand out of Linda's grip.

Linda shook her head violently. "No, I don't believe you. If you'd really met him, you'd know that he is just as miserable in this world as I am. He's a virtual prisoner in his castle in the clouds, along with all the others who couldn't adapt to this world. He didn't want me to have that life. He sent me away out of love. But I found a way for us to be together again!"

"The Wild might take the world, but it won't take the clouds." She thought of the vines she'd seen crawling over the giant's castle and knew she was lying. The Beast and his creatures could never have held out against that on-slaught. But Linda didn't know that. Julie remembered how her dad, his voice filled with certainty, had charmed the policeman outside Graceland. She needed to be *that* persuasive. She needed a hero's charm. "He has teams of creatures chopping down beanstalks as soon as they appear," Julie said. "I watched them. They used ropes to lower themselves down far enough to hack down the stalk. They used fire to burn them to the ground." With as much confidence as she could manage, she said, "You'll never be with your Beast. You *lost*."

Julie had never seen someone destroyed by words before. Linda's knees buckled, and she sank down onto the floor. "While you made your way to the well, the Wild talked to me," Linda said. "He said if the new stories didn't work, if the world didn't change enough to allow the Beast to come down from his clouds, then he had a plan. The Wild would release the prince, and I would set the traps. The Wild promised it was the perfect plan."

"The Wild used you," Julie said.

"I cannot live without my Beast," Linda said, her voice shrill. "I tried. I truly tried to start anew, to live in the world like he wanted me to, but I can't be without him."

The heartbreak in her voice . . . it shook Julie. She almost wanted to apologize, to tell her the truth—that the Beast had been moments from losing to the Wild when she left and was certainly back in his fairy tale by now.

"I am meant to love him," Linda said. "I was made to love him, and he was made to love me. Why does he fight this? We were going to be together. He was supposed to love me enough to want to be together." She sounded so lost.

All Linda wanted was her Beast back. Julie could understand that. Hadn't she just crossed the entire United States chasing her father? "The Wild *used* you," Julie repeated. Linda wasn't the true enemy. Bobbi wasn't the enemy. The birds in Times Square, the wolf at Graceland, the dragon in the Grand Canyon . . . None of them were the real enemy.

The real enemy was the Wild. And it was coming.

As Linda began to cry, Julie spotted a fire extinguisher next to the makeup counter. She picked it up and aimed the nozzle at the nearest swan-man. "I'm not your enemy either," she said to him, "but I want my family." Even if it was only for a few minutes, she wanted them all to be together when the Wild came. When the swan didn't move, Julie sprayed. The swan-man squawked as white foam hit his face.

Boots darted out from between the swans and ran to Julie.

Without hesitating, Julie turned and bashed the door with the bottom of the fire extinguisher. After three hits, the door popped open. A frog hopped forward. "Dad!" Julie cried. She scooped him up and hugged him, pressing her cheek against his cool, rough skin.

"Ribbet!" he said.

Inside the closet, she saw empty shelves—and at the very end, under a window, in a pool of light cast by the floodlights outside the castle, she saw Mom. In the light, her wheat-colored hair gleamed.

Duct tape was plastered over her mouth. Julie ran forward. "Mom, are you okay?" She pried the corner of the duct tape off with her fingernails. "Sorry," she said as she yanked the duct tape off as quickly as she could.

Her mom gasped. Her face was blotchy where the tape had been, and strands of glue residue hung from her cheeks. "Julie!"

"Hold on, I'll get you loose," Julie said. She placed her frog father on Mom's lap and then knelt down behind the chair and began to tug at the knots in the rope.

Squirming in her chair so she could see Julie, Mom said, "That's twice now that you've come to rescue me. Once is chance, but twice is a pattern. You've become a hero, like your father."

Julie felt herself blush. A hero. She wasn't a hero. She wiggled the knots, and the rope slipped a few inches. Beneath the rope, her mom's skin was red and raw. She guessed that Mom didn't know about all the fairy-tale events that Julie had failed to stop. Mom wouldn't have called her a hero if she knew about them . . . unless, of course, she hadn't meant that as a compliment. As a hero, Dad had caused at least as many problems as he'd solved. The knot fell open, and Mom wriggled her hands out.

"How bad is it?" Mom asked, gingerly massaging her wrists. "Where are Linda and Bobbi? Where are Boots and your grandmother?" Dad leaned his frog head against Mom's arm, as if to comfort her.

Boots leapt up onto her lap. "Well, we have good news and bad news. Good news is that I'm here. Bad news is . . . so's the Wild."

"Nearly here," Julie corrected. They had a few minutes, maybe. "There's time for you to kiss Dad and turn him back into a human. We can face the Wild together."

Mom shook her head as her fingers continued to pet Dad. "I won't add to it," Mom said. Her eyes were bright with unshed tears. Maybe she didn't understand how much the Wild had grown, Julie thought. She didn't know how hopeless it was.

"It's nearly to California already," Julie said. "What difference does one more fairy-tale moment make? Please, Mom, I want us to be together when it comes." Maybe it wouldn't matter if they were together as themselves or not, but it felt like it *should* matter.

Mom shook her head. "Even so. I'm sorry, Julie, but I can't. Your father understands."

No, she thought, he doesn't understand. She thought of how he'd chased after Sleeping Beauty. She thought of how he'd killed the wolf. She thought of how he'd left her in the Grand Canyon . . . Dad didn't care much about consequences. If their roles were reversed, Dad would have kissed Mom without a second's hesitation.

And maybe that wasn't entirely wrong. Maybe Linda had gone too far for her love, but maybe Mom wasn't going far enough. Maybe there was a middle ground.

Julie lifted her frog-dad from her mom's lap and held him at eye level. She couldn't stop the Wild from coming, but she could bring her parents back together. She was going to reunite her family. She wasn't going to fail in that. "I'm sorry, Dad," Julie said. There were two versions of the frog prince tale. In one, a kiss from the prince's true love broke the spell. In the other, a princess threw the frog against a wall and broke the spell. Technically, Julie was the daughter of royalty. "But this is going to hurt a bit."

"Julie, no!" Mom cried.

Tossing underhand as if he were a softball, she threw her father against the closet wall. He hit with a splat. She shielded her eyes as sparkles flared. The shelves shook.

Suddenly, outside the castle, the floodlights went out.

"Oh, not good. The spell didn't do that," Boots said. "Why are the lights out?"

A thin pool of moonlight shone through the window

at the back of the closet. In that sliver of light, Julie saw a man, her father, upside down on the floor in front of her. "Your mother is right," Dad said as he untangled himself. "You have become a hero." He smiled at her, a thousand-watt smile.

Julie smiled back.

The window darkened as leaves sprouted over the glass. Green moss spread over the closet ceiling. Vines crept inside the broken window and snaked across the walls and onto the shelves. Sunlight poured into the closet as the Wild turned night to day.

Pale, her mom stood up. *"Run,"* she said.

## Chapter Seventeen
### *The Wild*

Julie, Boots, Zel, and Prince bolted out of the closet into the costume room. Run, run, run! Julie ordered herself. It's here, it's here, it's here!

Dad flung open the door—

With a thundering crash, trees burst out of the concrete in front of the castle door. "Dad!" Julie shrieked. Vines thickened and knotted around the trunks. Leaves unfurled, and pine needles burst into full array on branches. Julie stumbled back against her mom, and Mom wrapped her arms around Julie's shoulders. In two strides, Dad crossed to Mom and Julie and enfolded them both in his arms. Boots pressed against Julie's ankles.

For the first time ever, Julie's family was together. And soon, they'd be torn apart as the stories found them. She felt her heart thudding so fast and hard that it felt as if it was going to leap out of her chest. The same thought kept running around and around in her head: It's here! The Wild is here! The words were a roar inside her, matching the thunder of the newborn trees as they split pavement all around the castle.

In seconds, everything was still. Sunlight, tinged green by trees, filtered down into the castle. The only sound was Linda's crying. She hadn't even looked up.

Julie heard a soft pop. Sparkles swirled, and Bobbi suddenly appeared inside the cyclone of glitter. She held a shining wand with a star on top. She was wearing a pink tulle ball gown. Sparkles settled in her hair and lingered there like a crown of stars.

If she was here, what happened to Grandma? Grandma couldn't have lost their battle. Could she have? Was she all right? Had Bobbi hurt her? "Where's—" she began.

Mom clasped her hand over Julie's mouth. "Shh," she whispered in her ear. "Don't draw attention. She was summoned by Linda's tears. Tears bring the fairy godmother."

Giant butterfly wings fluttered on Bobbi's back, sending off another shower of sparkles. Smiling beatifically, Bobbi fixed her gaze on the sobbing librarian. "Why are you crying, child?" she asked in a sugar-sweet voice. "Do you wish to go to the ball?"

Linda's head shot up. She scrambled to her feet. "I'm not Cinderella! I'm Beauty! I want my Beast!"

"You must remember to return by the stroke of midnight,"

Bobbi said. She raised her wand. The sparks crackled, and she sighed happily.

"No!" Linda cried, and ran out the castle door. She plunged into the forest. Wings fluttering, Bobbi flew after her. Sparkles dripped off her wand like an overzealous firecracker. She disappeared between the sun-dappled trees.

Julie swallowed hard. "That was close," she said.

"Relief later; escape now," Boots said.

"The Wild's changing the castle," Mom said. She pointed to the wall. Paint peeled from the wall to reveal Gothic stone. Above, fluorescent lights morphed into chandeliers, and medieval torches popped out of the walls. "Everyone out!" She herded Julie and Dad toward the door. Boots bolted ahead of them.

"Wait," Julie said, pulling away from Mom. "We can't leave! There could be a door to the wishing well here!" She ran back across the costume room to the closet doors. None of them looked like the purple motel room door. She tried one door—it was unlocked, a janitor's closet. She tried another—locked.

"Stand back," Dad said. He ran at the door and bashed into it with his shoulder. It popped open.

Inside the closet, tied and gagged, Henry and his father struggled in side-by-side chairs. Rumpelstiltskin and Henry! Julie had forgotten them. She couldn't believe she'd forgotten them. "Help me!" Julie called to her parents.

Dad rushed forward, and together they set to work on the ropes.

"You!" Henry said as Julie removed his gag.

Julie blushed. Was that a good-to-see-you "you" or a why-do-*you*-keep-showing-up-when-horrible-things-are-happening "you"?

"I thought that dragon fried you!" Henry said. The words tumbled out of his mouth so fast that he sounded as if he was in fast-forward. "I saw the flames. It breathed fire! I thought it would drop me over the Grand Canyon. I thought I was dead. I thought *you* were so dead when you fell into the trees and the bath mat burst into flames and—"

"What!" Mom said, face pale. Quickly, Julie filled her in as she tugged at the knots binding Henry's wrists. She didn't look up at her mom as she tried to gloss over how Dad had left her— "You left her at the bottom of the Grand Canyon!"

Dad paused and looked up from the knots around Rumpelstiltskin. "I came to save you," he said to Mom. "I am your hero."

Mom clenched and unclenched her fists. Through gritted teeth, she said, "You're also Julie's father." Squirming out of the last of the ropes, Rumpelstiltskin rushed over to Henry. He helped Julie yank the final knot free and began checking his son for injuries. "If you want to be my hero, you will never, ever, *ever* abandon our daughter again."

Dad looked at Julie as if he'd never seen her before, and then he dropped to one knee in front of her. "Forgive me," he said. "I have failed you."

Julie blushed. She did not want her father to bow to her. "He saved me from the wolf," she said to Mom. "Would you have done that if it meant the Wild would grow?"

Mom hesitated for the barest second. "Oh, Julie, of course, I—"

Helping Henry stand, Rumpelstiltskin interrupted, "We need to leave this castle. Too many ways to be trapped in a castle."

"Where's Boots?" Julie asked. She looked around them. He'd been with them when Bobbi appeared. Had he come with them to rescue Rumpelstiltskin and Henry? She remembered seeing him run toward the door— "Oh, no, he's out there," she said. "He ran into the woods!" She ran out of the closet. "Boots!" Mom and Dad followed, also calling for Boots.

As they crossed the costume room, straw bubbled up from the floor like popcorn. It poured out of crevices in the wall and rained from the ceiling. Boxes and crates transformed into bales of straw. "What's going on?" Henry said, his voice a squeak.

Rumpelstiltskin marched to the spinning wheel and sat down.

"Dad, what are you doing?" Henry said.

Zel caught his arm. "He can't help himself. It's the Wild."

With robot-like precision, Rumpelstiltskin scooped up a handful of straw and fed it into the spinning wheel. His foot began to tap on the pedal, and the wheel began to whir faster and faster.

"Why is he spinning?" Henry cried. "What's happening? You have to make him stop! How do we make him stop?" Straw zipped through Rumpelstiltskin's hands, and gold flashed on the wheel. "You have to help him!" He seized Julie's arm. "You started this! Everything was normal and fine and good until I met you!"

Julie didn't know how to help him. The only way to stop the fairy tales was to stop the Wild, and the only way to stop the Wild was with a wish in the wishing well, but the well was thousands of miles away in Northboro. Unless the motel room door appeared, she didn't have any way to cross thousands of . . . Yes, she did! She had Jack's beans! She dug the bottle out of her pocket and spilled a bean onto her palm. "We can reach the well through the clouds!"

Mom dove for her hand. "No! You'll start a tale!" Zel grabbed the bean out of Julie's hand and chucked it out a broken window. And then she stared at her hand in horror. A second later, Julie realized why: she had thrown a magic bean out a window, just like Jack's mother did in Jack's tale. That was a fairy-tale moment.

"Quick! Out!" Mom cried. "Before the beanstalk grows!"

"But my father . . ." Henry said.

" . . . is lost." Mom propelled them out the door and into the sunlit forest.

As they ran through the woods, the Wild continued to transform Disneyland around them. Up ahead, pastel horses neighed as they detached themselves from the carousel and galloped through the trees. A mermaid splashed in a fountain. Julie saw a man with a blue beard, a white doe and a weeping woman, a girl in a red cape, an old peddler woman with an apple in her hand . . . Ahead of them, a gift shop transformed into gingerbread. Candy canes sprouted on either side of the door, and the windows crystallized into sugar. From somewhere, a witch cackled.

"My father's back there!" Henry cried.

Julie glanced behind her to see that the castle had tripled in size. It had sprouted seven more towers, and they all gleamed in the sunlight like mother-of-pearl. From one window, a woman lowered a cascade of wheat gold hair. Julie's heart skipped a beat. Not Mom, she told herself. It wasn't Mom. Not yet. Cackling, a witch sailed over the tops of the tower.

"Your father is Rumpelstiltskin," Mom said to Henry, grabbing his arm to pull him onward.

"I don't care!" he said, yanking away from her. "I won't leave him! He's my father before anything else. Nothing changes that."

Julie had said those very words to him back in the RV at the Grand Canyon. "He's right," she said. "We have to try."

Henry shot her a grateful look.

"It's too dangerous," Mom said. "A castle is the worst—"

Before she could finish, the witch dove down toward them. Both Mom and Dad jumped in front of Julie. Dad drew his sword, and Henry ducked as the witch skimmed low over his head.

"No, Dad, don't hurt Grandma!" Julie grabbed his sword arm.

Cackling, Gothel wrapped her arms around Mom's waist and pulled her onto the broomstick. "Into the tower with you, my girl!"

"Mom!" Julie yelled, diving toward them. She landed facedown on the pine-needle-covered forest floor.

Dad swung his sword at the witch as she and the captive Rapunzel soared past him. He charged after her, and then he skidded to a halt. He turned back to Julie. Crossing to her, he held out his hand and helped her to her feet. "I will not abandon you again," he said, but his eyes shifted to the trees.

Julie saw that his scars were gone. His cheeks were smooth now, as if he had never fallen from the witch's tower. She thought of how the castle had sprouted additional towers. The Wild was setting the stage for him to reenact his story anew, and she could see in his eyes that he wanted to do it. In his heart, he was Rapunzel's prince, just like Linda was the Beast's Beauty. "Go," Julie told him. "It's okay. It's what you want to do. Go be a hero."

Saluting her with his sword, Prince plunged into the forest. He was gone almost instantly. At least he remembered me this time, Julie thought. That thought made her feel a little better. But only a little. She watched Mom and Bobbi disappear, a black speck against the brilliant blue sky.

The forest fell silent.

And then Henry started talking again. His voice sounded like a stream, words tumbling over each other like water over rocks. It was kind of nice and comforting. At least this time in the woods, she wasn't alone. "This was supposed to be, you know, a father-son bonding trip. I am one hundred percent sure this is *not* the kind of bonding stuff Dad meant. We were supposed to hike, fish, do touristy things. Not get kidnapped by a dragon, tied up in a castle, and left in a forest infested by fairy-tale bears and lions and witches and stuff—and I would have said 'left in a forest at night,' except it seems to suddenly be daylight, which is totally wrong because it was night, like, two minutes ago." He paused to suck in air, and then he said, "Julie, are you okay?" She felt his fingers touch hers, and she jumped.

Instantly, she wished she hadn't jumped. Had Henry been about to hold her hand? She felt herself blush and had to think for an extra second about his question. Was she okay? The Wild was here, and everyone she cared about was once again trapped in its fairy-tale stories. Worse, it was (at least partially) her fault—she'd performed the final fairy-tale event that had fueled the Wild. "Not really," she said. "You?"

He paused, thinking about it, and then said, "Not really. I never suspected. About my dad, I mean. Not once. All my life, he was pretending to be someone else, playing the role of the ordinary dad. Makes me wonder: how much of my life is a lie?"

Julie didn't know what to say to that. She reached out and touched his hand. His fingers curled around hers. His palm felt warm and damp.

"So what do we do now?" he asked.

Julie looked back at the castle, shining and shimmering above the trees. It was their only hope. She was sure of it. They needed a door in a castle that led to the Wishing Well Motel. She took a deep breath. "We go back there."

He stared at her. "But your mom said—"

"My mom's not always right," Julie said. As she said it, she realized it was true. Running and hiding weren't going to keep her safe. "Besides, you want to free your dad, don't you? The Wild can only control someone during a fairy-tale event. Once your dad's done spinning, he'll have free will again. He can escape before the next story bit starts. That's how I made it to the well last time."

As they walked back to the castle, past a cat playing a violin and an oversized egg perched on a wall, she told him about her mom, her dad, and the door to the Wishing Well Motel. She also told him about how she'd instructed everyone in Disneyland to retell her story and how she hoped that would force the Wild to include a motel room door in its castles. "Even inside the Wild, people will still be able to retell it, at least until they reach a story ending. Once they reach an ending, they'll of course forget everything."

"How many times does the story have to be told before the door appears?" Henry asked. "A hundred? A thousand? A million? A trillion?"

Good question. Julie didn't know. Could she stay clear of fairy-tale endings for long enough? It wouldn't do any good for the door to appear if she didn't remember to walk through it. She repeated the worry out loud.

"We'll just have to make sure we don't get caught in any stories then," Henry said. "We'll watch out for each other. I've got your back and you've got mine." The Cutest Boy Ever was saying "we." Julie stared at him for an instant and then realized he was blushing. "I mean, if that's okay with you," he said.

"It's okay," she said quickly. "Definitely okay. We'll stick together."

He smiled shyly, and she was suddenly very, very

conscious of the fact that they were holding hands. She knew she shouldn't care about it right now, with the Wild all around them and her parents trapped and Boots missing, but she was holding hands with a boy! She glanced down—and saw that there was a sword in Henry's other hand.

Her breath caught in her throat. Oh, no. Oh, no, no, no. "Where did you get that?" she asked, though she knew the answer. A story had found him!

He looked down at the sword and blinked. "I didn't . . . It wasn't . . ." He lifted it, and it glinted in the moonlight. "Whoa, it just appeared! Things aren't supposed to do that. Why did it just appear?"

Julie stopped walking. Trying to keep her voice even, she said, "Probably so you can fight the dragon." Curled in front of the castle was the dragon from the Grand Canyon. Its iridescent scales glittered as it flexed its wings. It fixed its eyes on them, and its forked tongue flicked out like a snake.

"I don't want to fight a dragon!" Henry panicked. "It breathes fire. Don't you remember how it breathes fire? It almost roasted you!" He shook his hand as if trying to drop the sword. Julie jumped back as the blade sliced the air in front of her.

"It's blocking the castle gate," Julie said, dodging the sword tip. "Give me the sword." She'd caught the attention of the dragon in the Grand Canyon. She could do it again.

Right? "I'll distract it. You get inside, rescue your dad, find the door to the Wishing Well Motel, and then wish for no Wild. Okay?" She tried to take the sword from Henry, but his hand wouldn't unclench. Sweat beaded on Henry's forehead, and his body began to shake. The Wild had already chosen its new knight, she realized. It was taking control.

"I can't let go!" he said, fear in his voice.

Which fairy tale was this? Was Henry about to be the knight who slays the dragon, or was he about to be one of the knights who failed? Every story had the older sons or pompous knights who failed before the hero finally won. "You have to ride it out," she said, fighting to sound calm. "When the fairy-tale moment ends, you'll be free again." Please, please, please, let him be a knight who lives!

He didn't have the chance to reply. Like a puppet jerked by strings, Henry marched toward the castle and the dragon. He held the sword over his head with both hands.

Julie watched through the trees. "Be careful, Henry," she whispered. If he didn't know how to fight a dragon, would he automatically be the knight who failed?

The dragon swiped its tail at the boy. It slammed into Henry's stomach. He sailed backward and landed in the bushes. Henry! About to rush to him, she stopped herself. Best thing she could do was get inside the castle. She could save him if she could get to the well. Julie crept closer to the castle.

Henry shouted a challenge to the dragon as he leapt to his feet. The dragon snapped its jaws in response. The sound echoed through the forest.

She was only a few feet from the castle now. All he had to do was draw the dragon a little farther away, and she could run inside.

A big green leaf jutted out in front of her. Instinctively, Julie raised her hand to knock it away—and her hand grabbed on, and held on.

She tugged at her hand. It continued to clutch the leaf.

"Oh, no," Julie whispered. This wasn't a leaf from a tree. This was a leaf from a beanstalk, grown from the magic bean that Mom had tossed out the castle window! She felt her body move toward the stalk. Stop, stop, stop! Her body wouldn't respond. Her foot lifted up and stepped down on a leaf stem, and she began to climb.

Below her, Henry charged at the dragon. She heard the beast roar. No! She wasn't supposed to be climbing the beanstalk! She was supposed to be searching the castle for the door to the wishing well!

Controlled by the Wild, Julie scurried up the beanstalk as fast and easily as a spider on a web. Higher now, she looked out through the leaves and saw the castle. She was as high as the tops of the towers, as high as the banners that flew majestically in the wind.

From one of the tower windows, a stream of wheat gold

hair draped down over the stone. A man was climbing the hair. Dad. Dad was climbing to Mom.

Julie's hands and feet never slowing, she watched as her dad climbed in through the window. She saw her parents embrace, and she swallowed a lump in her throat. Had they forgotten themselves? Had they forgotten Julie? "Mom! Dad!" she yelled. "I'm here! It's me, Julie!" The wind carried her words away.

She wanted to cry. It wasn't supposed to happen this way! The Beast and his creatures should have chopped down this beanstalk. Julie should have been able to sneak into the castle. She should have found the door to the well.

Below her, the sounds of the dragon battle faded.

It's not over, she told herself. She wasn't giving up. The Wild could only hold her during the fairy-tale moment. Once she reached the top of the beanstalk, she'd be free. She could find Northboro and reach the Wishing Well Motel via beanstalk, the same way she'd made it to Disneyland. She was not, not, not giving up, even if she'd lost her family, even if she'd lost everyone in the world. She still had a chance. When the Wild released her, she'd be free to act . . . at least until she met the giant's wife and set off the next part of the story.

After a few minutes more, Julie climbed through the clouds into sunlight. The tip of the beanstalk curled into a leaf. She jumped onto the clouds and then realized she had control of her body again—the fairy-tale moment was over.

Julie shielded her eyes against the sun—it bleached the sky and reflected so brightly off the clouds that it stung her eyes. Across the clouds, she saw the giant's castle, now coated in the ivy of the Wild.

There was no trace of the battle that had taken place here just a little while earlier. She didn't see any fabulous fairy-tale creatures. No elves, no trolls, no flying horses, no giants . . . There *had* to be giants. Better get out of here before one finds me, she thought.

East. She needed east. Which way was east? She squinted as she looked toward the sun. Had the Wild changed it to morning or afternoon? Morning, she guessed. In the original Jack and the Beanstalk story, Jack climbed up the beanstalk in the morning, so it had to be morning here. She took off running in the direction of the sun.

Her side began to cramp, but she kept running. East, east, east. Ahead, Julie saw a gap in the clouds. Reaching it, she dropped to her knees to look down at the Wild-covered world. Below, the deep green forest of the Wild stretched in all directions. She jumped up and ran farther. She spotted another hole and looked down. Same green. A third hole. Identical again.

This was hopeless. It looked the same everywhere! How was she going to tell which part was Massachusetts, let alone Northboro?

Catching her breath, Julie looked back at the giant's castle . . . Wait a second, the giant's *castle!* Maybe it had a door to the wishing well! But . . . how could she get to it? If Julie approached the castle, she'd meet the giant's wife and set off the next fairy-tale event.

She had a choice: she could try to guess the correct hole in the clouds and just as likely end up in Maine or Florida as in Massachusetts. Or she could deliberately walk into a trap. She could intentionally insert herself into a fairy-tale scene in order to get inside the castle. In the next part of Jack and the Beanstalk, Jack begged for food, and the giantess brought him inside and fed him. Once inside, she'd then have to find the door before the giant chased her down the beanstalk and ended the story.

"Do I have a third choice?" she asked out loud.

She couldn't think of one.

Julie started walking across the clouds. Was this stupid? Maybe. But if she went down the beanstalk to the wrong place, there were thousands of stories waiting to trap her. Here, there was only one. If she was quick enough and smart enough . . . It's a good plan, she told herself. Dad had said she made good plans, like her mother.

A drawbridge as wide as a highway lay across the clouds. It was held by wrought-iron chains so thick that she couldn't have wrapped her arms around a single link. Reaching the drawbridge, she climbed up and walked down the wooden highway to the towering gate. She stared up at vast doors, carved from trees so large that they dwarfed redwoods. Gathering her courage, she raised her hand and knocked on the enormous door.

The door opened with a whoosh of wind, and Julie found herself facing boots the size of her mom's Volkswagen. The cracked leather was as craggy as a mountainside, and the laces were like steel cables. Looking up, she saw ankles with stubble as long as blades of grass. Even farther up, she saw the face of the giantess Gina, who was now restored to her original size.

Julie felt her mouth move on its own. "Please," she said. "May I have a bit of breakfast?" She recognized the line. It was the next scene in the Jack and the Beanstalk story. Too late to reconsider now, she thought. Please, let this work.

"It's breakfast you want, is it?" Gina said. Her voice boomed across the clouds. "It's breakfast you'll be. My husband is a giant, and he'll eat you with toast if he finds you."

"Please, I beg of you!" Julie said. "Some food to eat!"

"Very well," the giantess said. "Come with me." Gina welcomed her into the castle, and Julie's body automatically followed.

Inside the castle, she saw towering throne-like chairs at a massive stone table. On it were cobweb-coated candelabras as large as streetlamps. Above, she saw a vaulted ceiling with tattered bunting. On the walls were tapestries with pictures of knights and unicorns and princesses so faded that they looked like old black-and-white photographs.

It had once been beautiful, she could tell. Maybe even glorious. But now . . . it all looked faded and tattered. Why hadn't the Wild transformed it? What was it waiting for?

She had an awful thought: was the Wild waiting for *her*?

Gina laid a napkin the size of a blanket on the floor. On the napkin, she set a wedge of cheese twice as big as Julie. Julie felt her stomach rumble. A six-foot-tall slice of bread was laid next to the cheese. Her hand reached for a hunk of bread. She tore off a piece and brought it to her mouth . . . and abruptly the Wild released her.

Julie jumped to her feet. This story bit was complete. The giantess had welcomed "Jack" inside and fed "him" breakfast. Now that Julie had tasted the bread, she was free. About to run, she hesitated. She should try to free the giantess too. "Gina, do you remember who you are?" she asked.

The giantess smiled sadly at her. "Oh, yes, I remember it all: my home, my friends, my Jack . . . We were happy. We'd made our own happily-ever-after." Her voice broke on the last word.

"Great!" Gina was still free of the Wild too! "We're between scenes, so you can escape now. You can come with me."

"Escape where?" Gina asked. "The Wild has spread

everywhere, Julie. There is no escape." She sighed. "Now that you are here, the story will end, and I will forget that I even wanted to escape. It is hopeless. I am tied to the Wild. I can never be free of it."

Yes, yes, the Wild was awful, but they didn't have time to talk about it. Any second now, the giant would return, and the next scene would begin. Julie had already lingered too long. "Gina, I'm sorry," she interrupted, "but have you seen a motel room door? Purple paint? Number thirteen in gold?" As she spoke, she looked across the banquet hall and saw an archway framed in ornate banners. Beyond it, doors lined a cavernous hallway. That had to be it! The motel door had to be there! In the story she'd told at Disneyland, the door was in a corridor. Without waiting for an answer, Julie sprinted across the banquet hall.

"Are you looking for your brother?" Gina called after her. "He was here earlier, asking about the same door."

Julie stopped. Boots? Boots was here? He wasn't caught in a tale? "Is he still here? Is he okay? Where is he?" Gina pointed in the opposite direction from the archway to a half-open door. "Thanks!" Julie said as she hurried under the massive stone table. She trotted toward the open door and climbed over the threshold. "Boots? Boots, are you in here?"

Inside the room, she saw a mountainous shape, wreathed in shadows, rise from a chair. The giant! She scrambled out of the room as he began to shout. His voice echoed through the castle. "Fee, fie, foe, fum, I smell the blood of an Englishmun!" The torches quivered. Several shook so hard that the flames went out. Behind her, the banquet hall was plunged into shadow.

"Be he alive or be he dead, I'll grind his bones to make my bread!"

An orange streak darted toward Julie. It leapt at her and crashed against her chest. She stumbled backward as a ball of orange fur dug its claws into the front of her coat. "Julie!" Boots cried. "Get me out of here!"

She hugged him. "Boots! What are you—"

"Giant!" he shrieked. "Run!"

Holding Boots, Julie ran across the banquet hall. The giant's footsteps thundered behind her. With a sigh, Gina waved as Julie ran out onto the drawbridge.

"Oh, no, not again!" Boots cried. Digging his claws into Julie's shirt, he yowled. All of a sudden, something shiny and round shot out from his tail. It splatted onto the draw-bridge.

She slowed, glancing back, and saw an egg, a golden-shelled egg, now cracked open on the drawbridge. "Was that—"

"Yes! I am laying golden eggs!" Boots yelped. "Do you have any idea how humiliating—"

Julie nearly dropped him. He was laying golden eggs. In

the Jack and the Beanstalk story . . . This was a trap! Behind her, the giant roared, "Thief! Return my cat who lays golden eggs!"

"Run!" Boots shouted.

Julie leapt off the end of the drawbridge onto the clouds. Instantly, a beanstalk burst up in front of her. With Boots cradled in one arm, Julie fought her own body as her hand grabbed onto a leaf and her feet jumped onto the stalk. No, she couldn't be caught! She couldn't leave the clouds! The door was here! It had to be! All she had to do was—

She began to climb.

"Stop, thief!" the giant shouted. "Return what you have stolen!" The beanstalk shook as the giant climbed on to chase her. She felt Boots's claws dig into her shoulders as she climbed down faster and faster.

This couldn't be happening! She couldn't be caught in a tale! She had to find the door! She had to reach the well! "Giant!" she called up. "I'm not a thief! My name is Julie, and I'm—"

"Who you are doesn't matter." His words were so soft that she nearly didn't hear them above the rustle of the beanstalk leaves. "You're the one who is going to kill me."

She wasn't going to . . . Oh, no, she was. As soon as she reached the ground, she'd chop down the beanstalk. He'd fall. He'd die. And then he would return to the beginning of the story, without his memory, to relive it all again.

Julie fought harder. She didn't want to hurt him. He'd tried so hard to escape this. Stop climbing, she ordered herself. Stop, stop, stop! But her hands and feet kept moving.

"Let me go!" she cried to the Wild.

Did it hear her? Did it care? It wanted this. It *wanted* her trapped in a story. It had tried to make Linda trap her as Sleeping Beauty. Since that had failed, it was now trying to trap her as Jack. In fact, she thought, the Wild could have brought Boots to the clouds and kept Gina free precisely to trap Julie. And its plan was working! When Julie reached the bottom, she'd chop down the beanstalk, and the tale would end. Julie would forget who she was. She'd forget about the Wild and the door to the well. And then she would climb another beanstalk and chop it down . . . over and over and over—*forever*.

Her feet touched the ground, and she released the leaves. An ax suddenly appeared in her hands. Stop! she tried to tell her arms. Don't do this! He'll be trapped! I'll be trapped! Her arms swung the ax toward the beanstalk.

*Crack.*

She wanted to shout to the giant, to warn him. But her throat wouldn't work. Even if she could warn him, he knew even better than she did what was about to happen.

*Crack, crack, crack.*

Julie kept pounding it with the ax. Green bits sprayed off in all directions. Beanstalk juice splattered her face and stung her eyes. Her palms ached. Sweat prickled her fore-head and ran down her neck.

*Crack!*

She heard his voice drift down from above. "Goodbye, Julie."

And the beanstalk began to tip.

## Chapter Eighteen
### *The End*

The giant didn't scream as he fell, but Julie did. She heard her own voice echoing in her ears as she watched the beanstalk plummet toward the earth. Its leaves fluttered as it fell. He clung to it. She saw a glimpse of his face: no fear. Just . . . sadness.

And then the beanstalk crashed down. She heard a horrible, echoing smack.

Silence.

"The end," she whispered, and the forest vanished.

## Chapter Nineteen
### *Jack*

A girl stood on a moss-covered path with an orange cow beside her. Forest hemmed the path on either side. Branches stretched like arms up over her, blocking the sun except in narrow shafts of dust-speckled light. She looked behind her. The path curved behind a tree and disappeared into shadows. She didn't remember coming from there. She didn't remember coming from anywhere. She was simply here.

Do I live here? she wondered. Where is here?

Ow, ow, ow, she thought as her head suddenly began to ache. It felt as if someone was squeezing her brain. Trying to distract herself from the sudden pain, she listened to the birds singing in the trees. Most chirped and twittered, but a few were singing in English about springtime and love. How pretty, the girl thought. The pain in her head began to fade. "Pretty," she said out loud, and the pain disappeared entirely.

"I want to chase those birds," the cow said.

She laughed as she pictured the cow trying to climb a tree.

"It's not funny," the cow said. "They're making me hungry."

"Sorry," she said, and stifled a giggle. Maybe he could swat them with his tail.

"Stop laughing."

The girl was saved from having to respond by the appearance of a man in blue jeans and a tattered coat walking through the forest toward them. As he approached, he waved and said, "Good morning! Where are you off to?"

How could she know that? She didn't . . . Ouch, her head hurt again. "I'm going to market to sell our cow here," her mouth said. Aha! She had a destination!

"Sell?" the cow said.

Funny how she hadn't known about the market before she spoke. Her mouth had simply known what to say. "I could save you a trip," the man said. "How would you like to swap your cow for these beans here?"

"I'm sure I'm worth more than beans," the cow said in an irritated voice. He pawed at her leg with his hoof. "Don't do it."

The girl patted his neck. Of course she wasn't going to sell him for beans. He was her first friend. She felt like she'd known him a long time, even though she could only recall the last few minutes.

"Ah, but these are special beans!" the man said. "*Magic* beans! If you plant them, they will grow into a beanstalk that reaches right into the sky."

She didn't want a beanstalk that reached into the sky. Why would anyone want that? But her hand stretched out and opened. She frowned at her hand. Why had it done that? Again, as soon as she asked a question, her head throbbed. Grabbing her wrist, the man poured five beans onto her palm. The girl's fingers closed over them. She stared at her fist holding the magic beans.

"Nooo!" the cow said. "Don't sell me!"

The man threw a rope around the cow's neck.

"I do not need a leash," the cow said. "I'm not a dog. I'm a . . . Am I a cow? That doesn't sound right . . ." He continued to protest as the man led him down the path through the trees. Soon, they disappeared from view.

The girl stood alone in the forest with five magic beans in her hand. Birds warbled in the trees, singing of princes and princesses. Why did I do that? she wondered. She hadn't wanted to sell the cow. He had made her laugh. Maybe she could trade back.

Putting the beans in her pocket, she started walking in the same direction as the man and the cow. As she walked, she saw she wasn't alone in the woods. By a pond, a girl played with a golden ball while a frog wearing a crown watched. In a clearing, two children nibbled on the roof of a candy house. She saw an old woman with a basket of bright red apples, and she saw a girl in a red cape and hood picking flowers. A knight in armor rode past her on a white horse. "Excuse me," she called to him. "Have you seen an old man with a cow?"

He didn't answer, and his horse didn't slow. It was as if he didn't hear or see her.

Walking farther, she came across a woman in front of a small cottage. Her face was expressionless, her arms hung listlessly by her sides, and her head was tilted as if she were listening to the birds sing. Intending to ask about the man and cow, the girl headed for the house.

As she reached the front gate, the woman said, "Back so soon, Jack?"

Back? Had she been here before? And was her name really Jack? A sharp pain immediately shot through her head. Okay, okay, she thought, I'm Jack. "Yes," she said to the woman. Instantly, her head felt better.

The woman shepherded her inside. "I see you no longer have the cow with you. You must have sold him. How much did you sell him for?"

The girl Jack reached into her pocket and drew out the five beans. She held them out on her upturned palm. "Five magic beans," she said.

"Beans? Beans!" The woman's face contorted, and she clutched her head as if she were suddenly in pain. She raised her hand. Her arm began to shake. Tears sprang into the woman's eyes. And then suddenly her arm swung fast at the girl's face, and her open palm cracked against her cheek. "Take that, you stupid child!" the woman cried.

Run, the girl told her feet. Run! But her feet wouldn't move. Why wouldn't her feet move? Run!

"Take that!" The woman struck again.

Pain exploded on her arm and shot up her shoulder.

And again. "Take that!"

She dropped to her knees, and the beans clattered to the floor. "Stop, please, stop!" the girl cried. "I'm sorry!" She shouldn't have given her the beans. But the girl didn't have anything else. She plunged her hands into her front and back pockets, and she pulled out a wad of crumpled and stained paper. She held it up like an offering. "Here! Please! This is all I have!"

Ignoring the paper, the woman scooped the beans off the floor and threw them out the window. "Out the window with the beans! And you, to bed without supper." Yanking the girl to her feet, the woman shoved her toward a doorway.

Hugging the paper, the girl cringed away from her.

The woman's face contorted again. "I'm sorry," she whispered as she shut the door. "Sorry, sorry, sorry."

The girl stood alone in the room and blinked back tears. Her shoulder ached, and her face stung. What had happened? What had she done wrong? What was she doing here? As her head began to throb again, tears spilled out of her eyes. They rolled down her cheeks and onto the papers that she clutched in her hands.

She looked down. She held several sheets of folded paper, all with writing on them. Sitting on the bed, she unfolded them and read the first sentence:

*Once upon a time, everyone lived in a fairy tale . . .*

What was a "fairy tale"? As soon as the question entered her head, a sharp pain stabbed into her with such fury that she gasped. The papers fell out of her fingers and fluttered onto the floor. As soon as they landed, the pain subsided.

She looked down at the papers. *Everyone lived in a fairy tale . . .* The words echoed inside her. The pain in her head, she decided, wasn't much worse than the ache in her shoulder or her back. She picked up the pages.

Everyone, she read, lived in a fairy tale while they were inside the Wild. "The Wild," she said out loud. She knew that word! How did she know that word? This time, she ignored her aching head. The Wild, it said, was the essence of fairy tales. While you were inside it, you were a princess or a knight or a witch. You were Cinderella or Sleeping Beauty or Jack . . . Jack? But *she* was Jack, wasn't she? She read further. You could choose to do whatever you wanted with your fairy-tale life. If you didn't want to go to the ball, you didn't have to. If you didn't want to fall asleep, you didn't have to. If you didn't want to sell your cow for magic beans, you didn't have to. And then, whenever you wanted, you could exit the Wild and return to your ordinary life. The papers went on to describe an adventure with two girls named Gillian and Julie . . .

Gillian and Julie.

The girl gripped the pages so hard that the edges crumpled in her fists. She knew those names. But this story wasn't right. The Wild wasn't like that. The Wild didn't coexist in peace with the world. It was either reduced to a tangle of vines under her bed or it dominated the world. There was no middle ground.

The girl Jack . . . No, not Jack. *Julie.* She was Julie! Julie hugged the pages to her chest as the memories rolled back over her. Gillian had written this story back before Julie's dad returned, before Julie was eaten by a wolf, before she was chased by a dragon in the Grand Canyon, before the Wild swallowed her family . . . before the Wild swallowed everything!

Julie jumped to her feet. She knew what she had to do: (1) find a castle, (2) find the door, (3) find the well, and (4) make a wish—four steps, all of which had to happen before the Wild caught her again.

You can do this, she told herself. You're the daughter of Rapunzel and the prince—the daughter of a general and a hero. You have both their strengths. This time, you won't fail.

Step one: find a castle.

She knew exactly where to look. Rushing to the window, Julie threw open the curtains. Giant green leaves blocked the view. She shoved Gillian's story back into her pocket and raised the window. As soon as she did so, the Wild grabbed control of her. Her shoulder twinged as her arm reached for a leaf, but she didn't fight it. She wanted to climb. She *needed* to climb. Scrambling out the window, she latched onto the beanstalk. Her hands reached for leaf after leaf, and up she went. Julie climbed higher and higher until she was surrounded by thick white mist. Soon, the beanstalk narrowed, and without pausing, she stepped off the leaf to stand knee-deep in white fluffy clouds.

Julie had control of her body again, but she didn't stop moving. She marched across the clouds toward the castle. She climbed onto the drawbridge and then knocked on the vast castle doors.

Once again, Gina the giantess opened the door, and Julie felt the Wild take hold of her again. "Please," her mouth said, "may I have a bit of breakfast?"

"It's breakfast you want, is it?" the giantess said. Her voice boomed across the clouds. "It's breakfast you'll be! My husband is a giant, and he'll eat you with toast if he finds you."

"Please, I beg of you!" Julie said. "Some food to eat!"

"Very well," the giantess said. "Come with me." As before, Gina led her into the castle, laid a napkin on the floor, and gave her a human-sized wedge of bread and cheese. Julie automatically ate a bite, and then the Wild released her.

This time, Julie decided, she wasn't going to ask if Gina knew who she was. She wasn't going to try to save her. She was going to leave Gina in her story. She couldn't afford to lose the time. "I'm sorry," she said softly.

Step two, she thought: find the door.

This time, she wouldn't let herself be distracted. Boots might be here, again laying golden eggs, but she had to leave him in a story too. She couldn't try to find him. Without another word, she leapt to her feet and ran across the banquet hall to the archway that she'd seen before. It felt wrong, deliberately leaving behind her brother and Gina. She told herself that this was the only way to save them all. They'd understand later.

She wondered if this was how Dad felt when he chose to chase after Sleeping Beauty and leave Mom or when he chose to chase the dragon and leave Julie. Like father, like daughter, she thought.

It took her five very long minutes to cross the enormous banquet hall and another two very long minutes to climb over the threshold into the corridor. The hallway was lit with torches the size of bonfires. Orange light played over the faces of massive doors. Please, please, please, be here, she repeated to herself as if she could make the motel room door appear by sheer will.

Julie raced down a hall so wide that it could have been a freeway. Every door she passed was a towering slab of wood and iron. She needed a small motel room door that was painted a faded purple with a gold number thirteen in the center.

What if it wasn't here? But it had to be, she thought. She'd told her story to people. People had heard it, and then they'd retold it. She'd made it a real fairy tale. The door had to be here!

Julie nearly ran by it. In a corridor of colossal doors, the human-sized door was minuscule. If it hadn't been painted purple, she wouldn't have seen it.

Without hesitating, Julie threw it open. Behind her, she heard the giant begin to shout, "Fee, fie, foe, fum!" Julie plunged through the door. It shut behind her, and every-thing was suddenly silent.

Green vines brushed her arms as she walked forward. She pushed aside a screen of leaves and stepped onto the sidewalk in front of the Wishing Well Motel. It worked! She was here! All she had to do now was cross through the lobby into the backyard, find the well, and make a wish to destroy the Wild.

The bells on the lobby **door rang** as she pushed it open. All the lights were out. **Shadows fell** across the lime green sofas. She hurried across the lobby. The lobby's back door was locked with triple dead bolts, but she knew where Grandma kept the keys. She dug them out of a fake plant's pot.

"Do not do this," a voice said behind her. "Please."

She spun around to see Henry standing beside the registration desk. "You're okay! How did you . . ." She stopped. Expressionless, he stared at her. She took a step backward. His voice . . . it had sounded flat and empty, like the voice in her nightmares, like Boots's voice when the Wild had used him like a puppet to talk to her. "You're not Henry," she said. "I mean, you're *using* Henry. Like a puppet. Do you think I'm going to listen to you just because you're 'borrowing' his body?"

"Inside my forest, he can be your prince."

For an instant, Julie stared at him—the Wild in Henry's body, the Wild looking out at her through Henry's green eyes. The Wild could do it, she thought. It could arrange for her to be a princess in a fairy tale with Henry as her prince. Of course, they'd forget who they were once they reached their fairy-tale ending. And who knew what sort of awful things would happen to them before they got to happily-ever-after? "I'm glad you didn't let him get eaten by the dragon. Thank you for that."

"Oh, he was," the Wild said.

Julie's heart lurched. He was . . . But the Wild had brought him back, the same way it would bring the giant back to life, the same way it had erased the scars on her father's face so that he could fall from the tower into thorns over and over again.

If she didn't stop the Wild, Henry would be condemned to be eaten over and over again forever—or something else horrible would happen to him when the Wild made him her prince. She unlocked the three dead bolts.

"Please," the Wild said, "do not destroy me."

He sounded so soft and sad that she paused as she twisted the doorknob. "I'm sorry," she said. "I don't have a choice. It's you or me." If she wanted to continue to exist as herself—if she wanted to have her family back—then Julie had to put a stop to this, to the Wild, permanently.

"You need me," the Wild said. "I am your dreams. I am your wishes. Destroy me, and you will destroy stories."

"I'm sorry," Julie said. This time, she meant it. As Gillian was constantly pointing out, stories weren't all bad. Stories had wonderful, magical, beautiful things too, like pumpkin carriages and castles in clouds.

"Your world would be lost without me—dreamless, soulless, empty," it said. "Imagine your world without fairy tales."

What *would* the world be like without the Wild? Julie

thought of the riot in Disneyland and shivered. People wouldn't want anything to do with fairy tales now. If it was dangerous for fairy-tale characters before, now it could be deadly. They'd be hunted down. Julie would be hunted down. She'd told the truth. She'd even told people her name! How long would it be before people came after her?

She'd find a way to survive. They all would. They'd change their names, move away from Northboro, pretend they were entirely different people . . .

Dad was right—that wasn't the "freedom" that the fairy-tale characters had fought for. And it wasn't what she wanted either. She didn't want to hide who she was (or to literally hide like the Beast in the clouds). She didn't want to lie to everyone she met and live in fear that they'd figure out the truth about who she really was inside . . .

But destroying the Wild was *still* better than living in the Wild. As miserable as the Beast was in the clouds, he fought the beanstalks. As bad as the world could get, the Wild was still worse. Right?

Julie pushed open the door.

"Destroy me, and you will destroy your parents!"

She froze.

"If I am destroyed, all the fairy tales of your world will vanish," the Wild said. "No stories, no magic, no wonder, no dreams. Without fairy tales, there can be no Rapunzel, no prince, no witch, no Puss-in-Boots . . ."

He was lying. He had to be. It was a trick. She shouldn't

listen to another word. "Step three," she said, "find the well."
She marched outside. The door slammed shut behind her.

Outside, moss grew over the concrete wall. Ivy wound
around the barbed wire. She waded through the bushes
until her toes smacked into the base of the well. Clearing
away greenery, Julie exposed the well.

It was exactly as she remembered it: half in ruins and
moss-coated. She stepped up to the edge. A tattered rope
hung in the center of the well. The bucket had been lost
years, probably centuries, ago. Here she was. It was time to
make her wish and end the Wild once and for all.

And possibly end her parents and her brother and everyone else she loved? Could Julie risk that? The Wild could
be telling the truth. Her mother wasn't human. She didn't
age. Her brother was a talking cat, clearly not a natural oc-
currence. Julie thought of Grandma. Even out of the Wild,
she still had her witch powers. She was a living fairy tale. If
Julie destroyed all fairy tales . . .

"What do I do?" she said out loud.

She needed a different wish. She needed another choice.
But what? There was no middle ground between the Wild
and the world. You couldn't have both . . .

Could you?

Julie pulled out Gillian's story. Her heart thumped faster.
Could she have both the Wild *and* the world? Could they
coexist?

Right now, with the Wild as it was, that was impossible,

but she'd said it herself in Disneyland: "This is how we defeat the Wild—we *change* it." She'd been talking about a single story, but what if she changed more than that? What if she changed the Wild itself? She could do it. She had the power. She was at the wishing well. And here in her hands, she held a wish.

"Step four," she said. "Make a wish."

Leaning over the well, she dropped the story in.

The forest disappeared in a blaze of white light.

## Chapter Twenty
### After Ever-After

*Three months later . . .*

Julie led her family into the brand-new visitor center next to the Wishing Well Motel. She smiled at the wide, sparkling banner that read:

WELCOME TO THE FAIRY-TALE CAPITAL OF THE WORLD!

She was wearing a matching T-shirt.

Bright murals with scenes from fairy tales covered the walls. Pamphlets with titles like "A Day in the Life of Cinderella" and "How to Be a Wicked Witch" filled display bins. A gift shop (closed now, since the center wasn't open to the public until tomorrow) sold T-shirts, hats, mugs, tiaras, red capes with hoods, and cat-sized boots.

Beside her, Boots gasped.

Julie looked down at him. "What's wrong?"

"If you buy me those boots, I will never, ever ask you for anything ever again," he said. He pressed his nose and whiskers up against the glass. "Red suede with rhinestones!"

Julie rolled her eyes.

"You did tell the Thomases noon, right?" Mom said. "You don't think they changed their mind?"

Dad placed a kiss on the top of Mom's wheat gold hair. "You worry too much." He's right, Julie thought. Mom didn't need to worry so much. The Thomases would be here soon, and then they'd join the celebration. There was a lot to celebrate. Things were changing. All around the world, fairy-tale characters were slowly winning acceptance. A unicorn could walk down the street today, and people would stare but no one would panic. Okay, not many would panic.

Before Mom could respond, the door burst open. Gillian ran across the center and hugged Julie. "I can't believe I'm going in today!" she squealed.

Julie grinned back. "Me neither." Tomorrow the visitor center would open, welcoming ordinary people into the Wild on a daily basis. Already there was a long waiting list. But Gillian and her family were first, as thanks to Gillian for writing the story that had changed the world. "Everyone ready?" Julie asked.

"Can I hug the kitty?" Gillian's little sister, Rachel, asked as she beelined for Boots.

"No, you may not," Boots said, evading her.

"Mommy, I want a talking kitty!"

Julie led both families to a wide sliding glass door. She slid it open and felt a cool breeze on her face. She smelled rose and pine. In the distance, she heard the sound of a waterfall and the faraway echo of a violin. She stepped out of the visitor center and in between the trees. They walked down a pine-needle-covered path through the woods to a small sun-dappled clearing that used to be the first tee at the Juniper Hills Golf Course.

Grandma was waiting for them. She had ditched the witch's cape and instead wore her favorite purple sweat suit as she sat astride her broomstick. "Well, don't you all look good enough to eat," she said.

Gillian's parents clutched each other. "Is she . . ." Mrs. Thomas began.

"She's our guide," Gillian said. "Right?"

Grandma smiled at her. Julie had never seen her look so happy or so relaxed. She'd come into the Wild to create an alternative to the wicked witch. It looked like it was working. To Rachel, she said, "There's a gingerbread house at the end of this trail. Eat as much as you like. Just don't get any ideas about shoving any witches in any ovens. We're skipping that scene. Now run along, and I'll be there shortly." She patted Rachel's head. When Mrs. Thomas began to protest, Grandma wiggled her fingers at her. Sparkles spun around Mrs. Thomas, and her smart business suit transformed into a shimmering silver ball gown. "Be home by the stroke of midnight," Grandma told her. She then turned to Gillian's dad. "You look like you could use an adventure. Hold out your hand." He did, and she tossed him a magic bean. Turning last to Gillian, she handed her a pair of silken shoes. "Here are your dancing shoes, Your Highness. There are eleven other princesses by the lake waiting for you to join them." Gillian let out a yelp of delight, grabbed the shoes, and raced down the trail.

Julie watched as each member of Gillian's family disappeared into a separate story. Through the trees, Julie saw a beanstalk spurt up toward the sky. Gillian's dad began to climb it.

"Are you sure you don't want to join us?" Mom asked Grandma. Cindy, a.k.a. Cinderella, was throwing a ball in honor of the new Wild. All the fairy-tale characters (and their families) were invited to the celebration, but Grandma had declined the invitation.

Grandma made a face. "Who would dance with a witch at a ball?"

Dad bowed. "I would be honored. Julie has told me of your bravery in Disneyland. You saved my daughter at great risk to yourself."

"A few more minutes and I would've taken Bobbi down," Grandma said, but Julie could tell she was pleased.

Julie heard a soft pop, and Bobbi appeared in a shower of sparkles. She smiled beatifically. "Did anyone call—oh, it's you." Her smile faded. She raised her wand, preparing to vanish again.

Mom sighed. "Wait," she said.

"Tell me you're not going to make peace with her," Grandma said. "You are way too forgiving. Can't I just turn her into a frog instead?"

"*Mother*," Mom said. "Tonight is about celebrating living in harmony." Gothel rolled her eyes. Julie hid a grin. She was with Grandma on this one. Bobbi definitely deserved some time as a frog. To Bobbi, Mom said, "We are on our way to Cinderella's ball. We'd be honored if you'd clothe us appropriately." She held out her arms as if waiting to be measured by a tailor.

Bobbi clapped and skipped in place. "Ooh, yes! How would you like something with peacock feathers?"

"Only if I can eat the peacock," Boots said.

Julie whispered to Mom, "You really think it's a good idea to let her wave her wand at us?" She really, really didn't want to be a pumpkin tonight. All the fairy-tale characters and their families were invited to Cindy's ball—that meant Rumpelstiltskin and Henry. She did not want to be round and orange in front of Henry.

"Harmony, Julie. Think peace and kindness toward all others."

Now it was Julie's turn to roll her eyes. She glanced over at Grandma, who waggled her fingers meaningfully. Grandma was ready with the frog spell. That made Julie feel better.

The fairy godmother waved her wand in the air. Sparkles flew in an arc and then showered over Mom, Dad, Julie, and Boots. Julie felt her clothes shift as her jeans poofed out into a butter yellow skirt, and she felt a breeze on her neck as her hair swirled up into a neat pile of curls. Beside her, Dad was suddenly dressed in a prince's doublet and hose. Mom wore a floor-length blue ball gown, dotted with teardrop diamonds. And Boots . . . Boots wore a cat-sized tuxedo.

"Sweet," Boots said, examining himself. "Precious is going to love this." He licked his paw and then smoothed a tuft of hair between his ears.

Bobbi jumped up and down, her wings fluttering. "You need a coach now. Let me make you a coach! What kind do you want? Pumpkin, zucchini, apple, orange, pear, apricot, peach, turnip . . ."

Grandma wiggled her fingers at Bobbi, and all of a sudden a fat green frog hopped up and down on the forest path.

"Why did you do that?" Zel cried.

Grandma shrugged. "Fingers slipped."

Julie clapped her hands over her mouth to keep from laughing out loud. Glancing at her, Grandma winked.

"*Mother.*"

"I couldn't help myself," she said. "I'm the witch." And then she grinned.

"You'd better apologize," Mom said. She sighed and then gestured to Julie, Dad, and Boots. "We'll walk to the ball."

Waving goodbye to Grandma, Julie headed off with her family deeper into the forest. Birds swooped and sang over their heads, some of them chirping and tweeting and some of them singing in English. She heard at least one Italian aria and a few very bad rhymes.

As they walked through the trees toward a shining lake (formerly Bartlett Pond in Northboro), Julie heard the sounds of violins. When the trees parted, she saw a manicured garden with bowers of roses in every shade imaginable: ruby red, pastel pink, bright fuchsia, orange, yellow, even green and blue. In between the roses, she saw . . .

. . . pretty much everyone. Snow and her seven men danced in a circle around three billy goats. Little Red Riding Hood (who had flown in from France for the event) flirted with the huntsman (from both her story and Snow White's story). The Singing Harp from Jack and the Beanstalk climbed onto the stage with the violinists and sang accompaniment. When she stopped, a cat with a fiddle performed a solo. As Julie and her family approached, Mom's friend the childlike Goldie (a.k.a. Goldilocks) raised a glass of champagne toward them, then continued her conversation with a blonde princess. Julie scanned the crowd, looking for more familiar faces. Okay, looking for one familiar face.

Henry was supposed to be here.

Nervously, she fiddled with her dress. She hoped it looked all right. She hoped it didn't vanish at midnight and leave her in rags rather than her original clothes. She liked that pair of jeans.

"You came!" Gina the giantess boomed. She strode toward them. These days, she was eight feet tall (tall enough to turn heads but not so tall that she couldn't fit into her New York City apartment). Jack trailed behind her.

Zel hugged them both hello. "Have you come to spend time in the new Wild?"

Sleeping Beauty's prince and his fairy joined them. "Ooh, no, no, no," the fairy said. The prince put his arm around her and added, "Just came for the food."

"Did you try the puffs?" the fairy said. "The cow catered." She beckoned the cow over to them. "Everyone, tell her what a magnificent job she did."

"Moo," the cow said modestly.

"We've opened a vegetarian café in the city," Gina said. "Toast of the town right now. We need to get back right after the speeches."

"Cow has been named a 'chef to watch,'" the fairy said. "She specializes in milk shakes and vegetarian burgers."

"We named it the Cow Patty," Jack said.

Julie laughed. That was perfect!

"Classy, huh?" he said, and winked at Julie.

"Very," she said. She glanced again at the crowd of people (and elves and unicorns and Bo-Peep's sheep and the Goose Girl's geese, as well as the giant from Jack and the Beanstalk, who was telling stories to an audience of lions and bears). No sign of Henry yet. What if he changed his mind? She should have called and asked if he was coming, but would that have meant she was asking him out? What if he'd said no? Better to run into him casually here, if he came.

Off to the side of the ball in a gazebo, Julie saw two other people she recognized. One was unmistakable: a mass of shadows and fur, the Beast was like a dark cloud against a sunny sky. The other . . . "Is that Linda? I mean, Beauty," Julie said. "She came?" Regardless of Mom's "harmony" ideas, a lot of people here had definitely not forgiven her.

Jack nodded, solemn now. "Rumor has it that the Beast asked her. She wasn't going to say no to him."

"They're back together?"

"It's true love," Jack said, his hand closing around Gina's. "And a lot of hours in couples therapy."

"Don't worry," Gina said. "At the insistence of the farmer's wife, the Three Blind Mice are with her, listening for anything suspicious."

Boots's ears perked forward. "Mice?" Before anyone could

say a word, he shot off through the crowd of dancers. His tuxedo tails flapped behind him.

"Oh, great," Julie said. "I'll stop him." Hiking up her ball gown, she chased after Boots. "Boots, come back! You can't eat family friends!" She wove between the dancing trolls, bears, and elves. An orange streak, Boots zigzagged ahead of her. In seconds, she lost sight of him. She slowed. He knew he shouldn't eat talking mice, right? She shouldn't worry. Standing on tiptoes, she tried to see over the crowd.

A hand touched her elbow. "Julie?"

She twirled to face the speaker, and her gown swirled out around her. Henry, in khakis, a shirt, and tie, stood in front of her. Suddenly, she couldn't think of a word to say. "Uh, hi," she said. She took a deep breath, trying not to pant from her sprint across the dance floor.

"I've been looking for you everywhere!" Henry said. He *had*? Inwardly, she cheered. "We've been unpacking all week, and Dad has me fixing stuff. Kind of not so good with plumbing, we learned, so I'm not doing that anymore, but there are like a million things to do around the motel, and, anyway, that's why I didn't call."

"It's okay," she said, smiling. She hadn't really expected him to call. He and his dad had just moved to Northboro from New Jersey. Rumpelstiltskin had volunteered to run the motel (and watch the well) while Grandma was in the Wild. It was the least he could do, he'd said.

A waltzing bear (Gillian's friend, of course) bumped into Julie's back, propelling her forward. Henry caught her arm. "You all right?" He paused and blushed. "Um, did you want to dance?"

Now it was her turn to blush. "Sure."

He put his hands on her waist, and she put hers on his shoulders. After a second's thought, he took one of her hands and held it out stiffly to the side like the waltzing couples around them were doing. He didn't try to waltz. Instead, they swayed from side to side.

A prince and princess swirled past them in elaborate figure eights. The prince dipped the princess. Julie saw Henry glance at them and then gulp. Before Julie could say that he didn't have to dip her, that this was fine (better than fine—she was dancing with the Cutest Boy Ever!), a voice yodeled across the dance floor. "JOOOO-LIE!"

Wincing, Julie looked over to see Cindy waving at her. Julie raised her hand and gave a halfhearted wave back. Cindy wore a knee-length sequin dress and had her hair in six or seven pigtails at odd angles over her head. Clearly, she hadn't let Bobbi wave a wand at her.

Cindy gave her two thumbs up. "You're dancing with a boy!"

All the nearby characters turned their heads to look at her.

Julie felt her face burn. Out of the corner of her eye,

she saw that Henry was blushing too, up to the tips of his ears. She couldn't look directly at him. "Do you want to, um, go for a walk or something, you know, not here?" she mumbled.

Henry nodded fervently.

Julie led him across the dance floor. All the dancers parted for them, letting them pass, watching them as they passed.

"Maybe we could walk faster?" Henry suggested.

"Or fly," Julie said. "Wild, I know you can hear me . . ."

Half a minute later, a dragon with mother-of-pearl seashell-colored scales and golden wings soared over the forest and then sailed over the lake to land directly in front of Julie and Henry. Julie grinned. "Thanks, Wild."

"He's not hungry, is he?" Henry asked Julie. "'Cause I really, really, really don't want to be eaten again." He shuddered. "You don't know what it was like."

"Actually, I kind of do," Julie said. She smiled at him. Finally, she'd stopped blushing. "Come on. I promise he won't eat you."

He grinned. "Wow. Yes. Cool."

Turning, Julie waved at her mom. "We'll be back soon!" she called.

Mom was holding Dad's hand. She'd pretty much been holding Dad's hand constantly for the last three months. "All right! Be careful!" Julie saw her turn to Dad and ask him something. His face lit up in a smile. Mom called to Julie, "If we're not here, we'll be in the tower!"

Julie climbed on the dragon and sat near the base of his neck. Henry settled down on the dragon's back behind Julie. He wrapped his arms around her waist to hold on. She felt her heart beat faster. The dragon began to flap his wings, churning the wind. Leaves fluttered on the trees, and the dragon lifted into the air.

As they rose above the Wild, Julie saw the swathe of green forest that now occupied the southeast corner of town, covering both Bartlett Pond and the former Juniper Hill Golf Course. She watched the trees undulating, remaking themselves. To the north, she saw a gray stone castle. A half mile south, she saw a glass hill. A beanstalk rose to the clouds.

Wow, it was all beautiful. Seeing it, she couldn't imagine that the Wild had once been a mat of vines under her bed (though she definitely appreciated having her room back). Julie laid her cheek against an iridescent scale and listened to the thrum of the beating wings. The sun was warm on her back, and the wind streamed through her hair as they flew over the Wild.

"How far can he fly?" Henry asked.

She knew what he was asking: could the dragon fly out of the Wild? She grinned. "He can fly anywhere now." To the dragon, she said, "Go on. You can do it."

In answer, the dragon shot forward. They zoomed over the trees—and then suddenly, as if it weren't momentous at all, they flew out of the Wild and over Northboro. Spreading his shimmering wings, the dragon soared over houses, rocketed above the highway, and swung around a shopping mall. Julie turned to grin at Henry. His face was inches from hers and she was suddenly conscious of how very green his eyes were.

As the dragon flew higher, Julie leaned just an inch toward Henry. And then, high above the clouds, he kissed her. It was, she thought, the perfect fairy-tale ending.